"Nobody move!"

Slowly Julie turned around

Incredibly, she found herself staring right at . . . herself!

It wasn't a mirror image of herself—not exactly. For one thing, the other Julie wasn't wearing pajamas, but rather a pink bathrobe with a towel wrapped around her head. She also had dark bags under her eyes.

Still, she looked a *lot* like Julie. Like an identical twin, in fact. Same face, same body—even the exact same freckles on her nose (but not the same posture: this girl slouched badly). As for the dark circles under the girl's eyes, Julie often looked almost that bad in the mornings after the worst of her nightmares.

"Oh boy," muttered the boy. "Now we're in for it."

DREAMQUEST

Tales of Slumberia

BRENT HARTINGER

A TOM DOHERTY ASSOCIATES BOOK

NEW YORK

DREAMQUEST: TALES OF SLUMBERIA

Copyright © 2007 by Brent Hartinger

Reader's Guide copyright © 2008 by Tom Doherty Associates

A Starscape Book
Published by Tom Doherty Associates, LLC
175 Fifth Avenue
New York, NY 10010

www.tor-forge.com

ISBN-13: 978-0-7653-5263-7
ISBN-10: 0-7653-5263-X

First Edition: May 2007
First Mass Market Edition: May 2008

Printed in the United States of America

0 9 8 7 6 5 4 3 2 1

For Michael Jensen

CONTENTS

Julie's Nightmares

JULIE FRAY stood in the center of a giant black and white chessboard. Game pieces as large as statues loomed up on either side of her. There were neat rows of white soldiers and nobles and knights on one side of the board, black ones on the other.

A horse whinnied—the mount of one of the white knights. Then rosary beads clacked around the neck of one of the black bishops.

These weren't statues, Julie realized. They were living, breathing beings!

"Pawn to queen's rook five!" said a voice.

It was the white queen, standing on the top of a small white dais. The voice sounded familiar.

"Mom?" Julie said. "Is that you?"

"I said," spoke the queen, "pawn to queen's rook five!"

It was her mother, dressed and painted like the white queen.

A different voice rang out from the opposite side of the chess board. "Pawn to king's knight four!"

Julie turned. "Dad?"

It was her father, made up like the black king, standing on a dais of his own.

"Pawn to king's knight four!" he repeated.

Julie's parents were talking as if she were the pawn to be moved around the chessboard. But they were demanding that she go in two different directions at the same time!

"Are you guys talking to me?" said Julie, feeling forlorn, glancing back and forth between her mother and father.

"Pawn to queen's rook five!" commanded the queen.

"Pawn to king's knight four!" demanded the king.

"Stop it!" said Julie. "I can't go to two different places at the same time!"

"Well, you certainly can't stay where you are," her mom said matter-of-factly.

"Oh, no," her dad said. "Whatever you do, you definitely can't stay there."

"Why not?" Julie asked uneasily. She couldn't remember the last time her parents had agreed about anything.

Before either of her parents could answer, the chess pieces all around her suddenly sprang into action. The pawns raised their pikes, the bishops drew their daggers, the rooks aimed their arrows, and the knights, sitting atop suddenly snorting horses, lowered their javelins. All at once, they bore down on Julie for attack.

As the pikes and daggers and javelins and arrows flew at her, Julie screamed. Then they hit. She expected pain. What she got was a sudden jolt.

And then she woke up.

❩

Julie shambled, zombie-like, into the kitchen. Her mother toiled at the stove, and her father sat glumly at the table eating breakfast and rustling his newspaper.

Her father spotted her first, and immediately brightened. "Julie!" he said. "Good morning!"

Her mother perked up too. "Julie!" she said, welcoming her like a restaurant hostess. "Come have some food!"

Julie hesitated, glancing down at the kitchen floor. The pattern of the linoleum was one of black and white squares—exactly like the chessboard of her dream.

Her stomach clenched.

"I'm making pancakes and orange juice," said her mother, holding up the glass pitcher. "The secret to making it taste more like fresh-squeezed is to mix the juice of a real orange into each glass of frozen concentrate."

Julie's mother was a product demonstrator. That meant she spent her days standing at little tables at the ends of the aisles in supermarkets, explaining various products. It also meant that, even at home, she tended to do everything very deliberately, often reciting household hints as she did so.

Julie took a seat at the table across from her dad.

"So!" he said to her. "You ready for that screening on Saturday afternoon? It's a rough cut, but I heard the rushes were terrific." Julie's dad worked as an executive at a television studio, which meant he was always using terms and expressions that Julie didn't understand. He also often took Julie to parties and premieres for new television shows.

"Oh, I'm sorry!" said Julie's mother, still standing by the stove. "On Saturday, I made plans for Julie to go with me to a blender convention. There's a new model that actually mixes food on the molecular level!"

The newspaper crumpled under Julie's father's hands. "You can't do that! Julie's busy with me on Saturday."

"It's a very popular convention," Julie's mom said oh-so-sweetly. "I had to reserve weeks in advance." She dropped a dollop of pancake batter onto the skillet, where it sizzled loudly.

"You *knew* Julie and I had plans for Saturday!" Julie's dad said. "You made your plans on purpose!"

"Don't be ridiculous! I just know how interested Julie is in frappéing."

Finally, Julie spoke up. "I can't do either of those things on Saturday," she lied. "I was going to spend the night with Lisa, and—"

"You are *not*!" snapped both her parents together.

"She's coming with me to the blender convention!" her mom said.

"She's coming with *me* to the rough-cut screening!" her dad said.

Julie's father and mother were so completely different that she often wondered how they had ended up together in the first place. Had they once loved each other? Maybe so, but after fourteen years of marriage, they now hated each other very much.

And as usual, they were putting Julie right in the middle.

)

THE TIME she spent at home with her parents was bad, and her sleeping hours were worse. But there was one part of Julie's life that was almost manageable: school. For six hours at least, she didn't have to deal with either bickering parents or horrifying nightmares. Plus, she got to see her best friend, Lisa Pituro.

In second-period science class, Julie and Lisa checked on their lima bean, which they'd been growing in a Styrofoam cup as part of an experiment.

"It's dead," Lisa said. "How can anyone kill a lima bean? It looks bloated *and* withered. How did we do that?"

"Too much water and too much sun," Julie said. "Too much of everything, I guess."

Lisa's eyes weren't on the dead lima bean. "You know, you don't look so hot either," she said.

Julie tried to shrug it off. "No, I'm okay."

"You had another nightmare, didn't you?" Lisa was the one person Julie had told about her horrible dreams.

Julie sighed. She'd never been able to lie to Lisa.

"It was terrible," Julie said.

"And your parents?" Lisa asked.

"They're terrible too. I don't know why they can't just fight between themselves. Why do they always have to bring me into it?"

"Gosh, Julie, that's rough."

"I could almost handle my parents' fighting if only I didn't have to deal with the nightmares at night," Julie said. "But the way it is, it's like I never get a break. It's just too much."

Their teacher, Ms. Ely, stopped by their workstation to check on their lima bean. She peered into their Styrofoam cup.

"Hmmm," she said. "This doesn't look so good."

"I think we got a bad bean," said Julie.

"I think you should have listened closer to my instructions," said Ms. Ely.

The teacher walked on, but in the back of the classroom, two girls burst into giggles. It was Veronica Sutton and Ashley Gold, the two most popular girls in class. It went without saying that they were laughing at Julie.

)

SHE LAY on her back on a great silver tray on top of a table spread with a crisp white tablecloth. There was an apple in her mouth and a row of pineapple rings around her whole body. Candles flickered in a nearby candelabrum—the only light in the darkened room.

Julie tried to move, but found she couldn't lift a finger. She couldn't even blink.

Figures emerged from the darkness. They were her parents, her mother on one side of the table, her father on the other.

Julie tried to speak, to call out to them for help, but her lips would not move.

Her parents were holding ceramic plates the size of garbage can lids.

"Oh, my!" her mother said. "Doesn't this look wonderful? Now, let's see. Do I want a leg or a thigh?"

Her father eyed Julie's torso hungrily. "Me, I've always been partial to ribs."

They're going to eat me? Julie thought.

No! She tried to scream, but still couldn't move a muscle.

Holding her plate in one hand, her mother brandished a glistening ten-inch knife. Her father, meanwhile, put his plate aside and held up an electric knife, the kind you use to carve a turkey. Holding it in both hands, he flicked it on, and it buzzed like a dentist's drill.

"Julie?" her father said. "Wake up!"

)

SHE AWOKE with a start. "Huh?"

Julie was lying on the couch in her father's bungalow at the television studio where he worked. She'd come here after school like she always did, so he could drive her home. She'd fallen asleep and had been right in the middle of a dream.

"You okay?" he said, concern in his eyes. "You looked like you were having a nightmare."

"No," said Julie, flushed, pushing herself upright. "I'm fine."

"Hey," he said, "you wanna hear this great idea I have for a new TV show?"

"What?" Julie said. "Oh, sure." The concern was already gone from his eyes, and that cut her as deep as any electric knife.

"It's a sitcom about a family," he said. "But it won't be actors playing the parts, it'll be the members of a real family!"

"That's not a new idea," said Julie, rubbing her face. "That's been done lots of times."

"Yeah, but this time, the family will also have a dog!"

Julie nodded. She had learned long ago to just listen whenever her dad was excited about some new show.

"You should see the actress we cast as the daughter!" he said.

"Actress?" said Julie, confused. "I thought you said you were using a real family."

"Oh, not a *real* real family. They'll be actors, but they're *playing* a real family playing a sitcom family. And I tell you, this actress is fantastic. *Hollywood Reporter* says her Q-rating is gold bar in the eight-to-twelve fem demo!"

More Hollywood talk. As always, Julie had no idea what he was saying.

While her dad jabbered on about the show, Julie stood up and walked to the window of her dad's bungalow. From there she could see the television studio outside. Rising above the whole facility was a big water tower. And spread out below that was a collection of huge warehouselike buildings, called soundstages, where they filmed or taped the various television shows.

Just across the way, the door to one of the soundstages stood open, and Julie could see inside. Technicians in blue jumpsuits bustled around the interior, adjusting cameras and lights that were all focused on a set made up to look like a typical family room.

Julie hated the television studio where her dad worked. Absolutely everything here was fake: fake conversations, fake family rooms, fake families. And yet, what happened out in that land of make-believe was far more interesting to her father than anything real, anything happening in his own real family.

"Now, your mother distinctly said not to spoil our dinners tonight," Julie's dad was saying. "So what say we stop somewhere for a little snack on the way home?"

❭

THAT NIGHT after dinner, Julie's parents had the television on in the family room.

"I think Julie would like to see our new show with the animated pandas," her dad said. "The above-the-line is almost nothing, and the back end is unbelievable!"

"*I* think Julie would like to see that show where the CEO trades places with the housewife," her mom said. "I still can't believe he didn't know the difference between delicates and permanent press!"

What Julie wanted—and what she told her parents—was to go to bed early.

"A simple hot-water bottle can warm the coldest of beds!" her mother called after her. "And unlike an electric blanket, it won't dry your skin."

Julie's bedroom had a big picture window that looked over the city. Before the nightmares, she used to sit at that window and stare out at the very occasional rainbow, or at whatever she could make out of the stars in the smog-filled sky. The room also had an actual wardrobe, something that had been in her family for years.

But Julie ignored all that and stood with her back against the inside of the door. She couldn't even bring herself to cry. It was like she was dead inside, cold and unmoving.

An antique looking-glass, a gift from an aunt, hung on the far wall, and in its reflection, Julie caught sight of her diary amid the clutter on top of the dresser. She knew she should write in that diary, but what was the point? She'd written the same words so many times before.

She could no longer handle being caught in the middle of

the war between her parents. But what could she do? They were the parents, she was just the kid. Her parents weren't even aware anymore of how much they fought. She had even heard them say they were staying together for her sake, like they were doing her this big favor.

And now there were the nightmares. What she'd told Lisa at school was the truth: she'd be able to handle her parents if she at least had a little peace at night. But now the situation with her parents had even invaded her dreams. And there didn't seem to be any way to change that either. How would a person go about changing her *dreams* anyway? Dreams weren't like television shows where you could just change the channel. Dreams were like parents, where you didn't have any control whatsoever.

Julie was eleven years old, with a smattering of freckles on her nose and shoulder-length chestnut hair that sometimes channeled the spirit of a willful four-year-old.

She was also quickly going insane.

Right then, it seemed like even one more night of nightmares might be just enough to cause her mind to snap completely.

Julie shuffled slowly across her floor. She was exhausted, so she dressed for bed and lay down in the sheets. But she didn't dare close her eyes, because she knew that sleep would only bring her yet another horrible dream.

2

Awake in Slumberia

S HE WAS lost in the strands of a lime-green shag carpet. Julie had somehow become very, very small, and the carpet fibers now surrounded her like the trunks of ancient trees. Jagged black boulders littered the ground around her—tiny granules of dirt to a normal-sized person.

A high-pitched whine penetrated the fibers.

She looked up. Through the looming carpet strands, Julie saw a towering giant in white tennis shoes. It was her mother pushing a vacuum cleaner.

"I'll do this room," her mother said in a voice that boomed out even over the thrum of her vacuum.

But then a second giant entered the scene. It was her father, pushing a vacuum of his own, this one with a low, even growl.

"No," her father said. "I'll do it. You do the bedrooms."

Julie knew if either of her parents vacuumed over her, they would suck her up like so much loose lint. If she didn't get torn to pieces by the suction, she'd suffocate in the vacuum bag!

"Wait!" Julie called, jumping up and waving her arms. But she knew right away that she was way too small, that there was no way her parents would see or hear her, buried deep in the carpet as she was.

"I was here first," her mother said. "I'll do it!"

"Oh, I get it," her father said. "You don't trust me to do a good job."

And then, gears grinding and bristles churning, the dueling vacuums were heading right for Julie. A moment later, darkness fell over the shag carpet, and the machines sucked furiously at the strands around her, which buckled like palm trees in the grip of a hurricane. The boulderlike particles flew up through the air, buffeting her.

"No!" Julie screamed. She tried to grab on to one of the lashing carpet strands, but she couldn't get a handhold.

Then she was flying through the air, twisting in the wind, being sucked toward two vacuums at once. The fury of the two motors was ripping her apart.

But at the exact instant before being torn open, Julie hit something solid, and the impact resounded with a loud metallic clang.

❱

JULIE GROANED.

She was clutching rivets at the top of some kind of massive metal tank. It was night, and a half-moon cast down a wan yellow light, but there were no stars in the haze of the sky, just like at home. The air smelled fusty, like an old couch. There wasn't the slightest rustle of a breeze.

Julie hurt all over. She had really hit the tank hard. The metal itself was cold, and Julie shivered. She was just wearing the pajamas she'd gone to bed in, with no shoes.

She pushed herself upright. The metal tank looked like the top of some kind of water tower.

Cautiously, she peered down. A cluster of buildings, arranged in rows, surrounded the tower. Some of the structures below were large and windowless, like warehouses. Others were smaller, little officelike bungalows. White trailers had been parked between the warehouses. A high concrete wall enclosed it all.

It looked a lot like her dad's television studio. Even the water tower was familiar.

What an odd dream this is, Julie thought.

For one thing, it didn't *feel* like a dream. It felt like she was awake. Even so, Julie knew it *was* a dream—or, rather, a nightmare. What else could it be?

A burst of noise below caught her attention: clangs and clicks and whirs and beepings. She leaned over the side but couldn't see anything. A metal ladder led down the side of the water tank. She crawled toward it and started climbing down.

Once on the ground, Julie glanced down the alleys between the warehouses. The area was deserted.

Suddenly a huge bird swooped low over her head. It

squeaked, but not like a bat—more like a rusted metal hinge opening and closing.

It flew under one of the lamps that hung from the warehouse eaves. In the light, it looked to be a tern or a gull, but one made entirely of metal plates, like a robot. A leather pouch hung from its underside. The bird was sleek and gracefully built, with a wingspan of at least three feet. But the flap of its wings was fast and labored, like it was fighting hard to stay aloft.

This is a very *strange dream,* Julie decided. What was this bird-creature anyway?

The noises Julie had heard—the clangs and clicks and whirs and beepings—were coming from inside the nearest of the warehouses. In the whole side of the building there were no windows and only a single door, which was open just a crack.

Suddenly the door jerked open the rest of the way, and a boy of twelve or thirteen stepped out. He was wearing a blue jumpsuit and lugging a huge coil of thick cord over his shoulder. He had dark skin, dark hair, and soft brown eyes.

He saw Julie and his eyes popped open. "Ms. Clavier?" he said. "What are you doing here so early?"

Julie frowned, confused.

"Really, Ms. Clavier," the boy went on, "why don't you go back to your trailer? I see you're already in costume, but we won't be ready here for a while yet."

The boy seemed harmless enough. But Julie knew that

looks could be deceiving, especially in nightmares. His innocent appearance could be a trick to get her to lower her guard. As soon as she did, he'd morph into a flesh-gorging mutant or a fire-breathing dragon. Still, it never did any good trying to outrun them.

"My name's not Ms. Clavier," Julie said quietly. "It's Julie. Julie Fray."

The boy clearly didn't believe her. "Look, Ms. Clavier," he said, "I have to get back to work, okay?" The boy glanced back through the open doorway behind him. Julie could now see into the warehouse.

It was definitely a soundstage, filled with lights and cameras, all aimed at a set made up to look like a hospital operating room.

There were people on the set, also in blue jumpsuits. They were the source of the mechanical noises Julie had heard. They were methodically adjusting the lights and rearranging the props and cameras, all without saying a word.

But the "people" in the soundstage looked very odd. For one thing, they were freakishly skinny and very tall—more like stick figures than actual humans. Their heads were even stranger: they were all hairless and perfectly round, easily the size of large beach balls. But it was also the way they were working, slowly and robotically, as if they had done these same things many times before.

One worker sidled past just inside the door. He glanced Julie's way. The skin on his head was tinted yellow and pockmarked, like the surface of the moon. But Julie didn't see any eyes or mouth or nose.

She looked back at the other creatures bustling around inside the warehouse. None of them had facial features!

She gasped. "What *are* they?"

"What?" said the boy, adjusting the heavy cables on his shoulder.

Julie pointed. "Those . . . *creatures!*"

"You mean the Moon People?"

She looked at him blankly.

"They work here at the dream-studio?" said the boy, as if prompting her.

Dream-studio? thought Julie. Things had started out getting curiouser and curiouser—but now they'd become downright bizarre!

She pointed into the soundstage. "What's going *on* in there?"

The boy sighed. "What else? Filming another nightmare. This dreamstage is being set up for the dream where Julie goes in for heart surgery. Her parents are both doctors, and they argue over who gets to do the surgery. They can't decide, so they end up both tearing her heart out."

Julie had to admit, that sounded a lot like one of her nightmares. But hearing the boy say it out loud felt like cold wind whistling through the wind tunnel of her soul.

"Something is very wrong here," Julie said, shivering.

"Why?" the boy said. "Did someone forget to order the fish guts?"

"Look!" Julie said impatiently. "I really can't take another shock right now, so if you're some kind of evil ogre in disguise, just go ahead and mutate, okay?"

Now the boy was confused. "What are you talking about?"

"You know what I'm talking about! I'm talking about this dream! I know this is another nightmare, so let's just get on with it, okay? Where are my parents? What horrible thing are they going to do to me now?"

"I don't understand," the boy said. "What do you mean, 'this is another nightmare'?"

"You just said that it was!"

"No, I said we're *filming* another nightmare. With the operating room and the fish guts? Ms. Clavier, this really isn't funny."

"My name's not Ms. Clavier! It's Julie!"

"Julie Fray?"

Julie nodded stubbornly. "That's right."

"But that's not possible."

"What do you mean? Why not?"

"Well, Julie Fray is just a character someone made up."

Julie had absolutely no idea what this meant. This dream wasn't quite as terrifying as her usual nightmares—yet!—but it was far more confusing.

"Look, I'm pretty busy right now," the boy went on. "If this is some kind of acting exercise, could you practice with someone else?" He turned to go.

"Please don't leave!" Julie pleaded. "I need your help."

The boy looked back at her. His eyes met hers as if for the very first time. His brow furrowed. He studied the rest of her face like it was a jigsaw puzzle, nearly complete.

"You're really *not* Vivian," he said at last. "Are you?"

"I don't even know who Vivian is. I also don't know where I am."

"Well, you're in Slumberia, of course."

"Slum-whatia?" Julia said.

"Slumberia. And this is the dream-studio, the place where they film the dreams."

The boy's words echoed in Julie's mind. But they still didn't make any sense.

"How did you get inside the studio anyway?" he asked.

"I don't know," Julie admitted. "I just found myself at the top of that water tower." She gestured back from where she had come. "I climbed down, and here I was."

"The creative juices tank?"

"The what?"

"It doesn't matter. What do you mean, you 'found' yourself at the top?"

"I was having a nightmare, and all of a sudden it ended. And then this one began."

The boy put down the heavy cables he was carrying and

squinted up at the water tower. "There's something up there."

Julie followed his gaze. A big black spot hung in the air above the top of the water tower. She hadn't noticed it when she was up there because it had been directly over her head. It was roughly circular, about two feet around. It reminded Julie of spilled ink, except it roiled ever so slightly.

"What *is* that?" Julie asked. "And how is it just floating in the air?"

"You tell me," said the boy.

"Wait a minute. You said that Julie Fray isn't real. She's the character in these dreams you're filming?"

"Well, of course. She's the *main* character."

Things were finally starting to make sense. Julie was dreaming about the place inside her own brain where her dreams were made—or, more accurately, "filmed."

But *was* she dreaming? Because it still didn't *feel* like a dream.

She pinched herself. Wasn't that what people were supposed to do to figure out if they were dreaming?

It hurt. But she didn't wake up. So did that mean this wasn't a dream?

Julie looked back at the black spot above the water tower. If this really was the place inside her brain where they "filmed" her dreams, maybe that was the way back into the rest of her brain.

"Well," Julie joked, "if this is where you film my dreams,

can I make a request? How about laying off the nightmares and giving me some happy dreams for a change?"

The boy sighed again. "Yeah, they're pretty awful, aren't they? That one yesterday where Julie's parents ate her? That was one of the worst yet."

"You *know* about that?" Julie said, taken aback.

"Well, yeah. I arranged the pineapple rings."

Julie's head throbbed. She had never had a dream before in which the characters knew what happened in her *other* dreams.

"If you thought the dream was so bad," Julie asked, "why didn't you stop it?"

"Me?" The boy snorted. "That's a laugh. No one ever listens to me. They just tell me what to do. I'm completely powerless."

"But—"

They were interrupted by an icy voice from directly behind. "*Nobody move!*"

Slowly Julie turned around.

Incredibly, she found herself staring right at . . . herself!

3

Confusion in the Dream-Studio

IT WASN'T a mirror image of herself—not exactly. For one thing, the other Julie wasn't wearing pajamas, but rather a pink bathrobe with a towel wrapped around her head. She also had dark bags under her eyes.

Still, she looked a *lot* like Julie. Like an identical twin, in fact. Same face, same body—even the exact same freckles on her nose (but not the same posture: this girl slouched badly). As for the dark circles under the girl's eyes, Julie often looked almost that bad in the mornings after the worst of her nightmares.

"Oh, boy," muttered the boy. "Now we're in for it."

"What do you mean?" Julie asked him. "Who is that?"

"Vivian Clavier. The actress who plays Julie."

"But *I'm* Julie!" said Julie. Even so, she finally understood how the boy could have mistaken her for this girl.

Vivian glowered at them from the open doorway of the largest of the white trailers. "What do you think you're doing, making all that *racket*?" she snapped. "Don't you know I'm trying to memorize my lines in here?" The voice was different from Julie's—louder and more shrill.

"Sorry, Ms. Clavier!" the boy said, hustling Julie along. "We were just leaving."

"*Wait!*" commanded Vivian. She frowned, squinting at them. "Who *are* you?"

"Uh, my name's Roman," said the boy nervously. "I work on the dreamstage."

"Not you, you idiot! The other one."

"I'm Julie—" Julie started to say, but Roman interrupted her.

"Ethan's niece!" he said. "She's visiting the dreamstage today!"

"Ethan's *niece*?" said Vivian, suddenly breaking into a huge smile. "Well, that's *different*! Why don't you come inside?" Vivian wasn't yelling at them anymore. Suddenly she sounded pleasant—almost sweet. She backed away from the doorway of her trailer, beckoning them in. "Come in!"

Roman whispered discreetly to Julie, "Just follow my lead, okay?"

It was a catastrophe inside the trailer. One-third of the room was taken up by an enormous makeup table with a massive mirror bordered by little lightbulbs. Jars and containers, most uncapped and some spilled, cluttered the table-top like a department store counter after an earthquake. Meanwhile, every other surface in the room was piled high with clothing—costumes, apparently. One mound was so high that Julie assumed there was a little sofa underneath. But nowhere did Julie see the script that Vivian had said she'd been so busy studying.

"Come in, come in!" Vivian beamed. "I'm so sorry about the mess. It's been one of those days. They actually had me being sucked up by these giant vacuum cleaners. Have you ever heard of anything so stupid? I was hanging from wires for two hours!"

Vivian had transformed herself. Julie felt like she was talking to a completely different person—someone completely relaxed and utterly charming. Even the dark rings under her eyes seemed to have vanished.

Vivian coughed. She reached for a bottle on the makeup table and took a drink. "Forgive me," she said. "My throat, it's so *dry*. I'd offer you some, but I'm afraid I don't have any glasses."

"That's okay," Julie said. "But about those dreams . . ."

Vivian smiled coyly. "Yes?"

"Well, they do sound pretty bad. So why not do different dreams? You know—something less nightmarish?" Julie still didn't know exactly where she was, or if this was all just another dream. But the people here in "Slumberia" did seem to know all about her other nightmares. So Julie didn't see how it could hurt to at least *ask* them to make different dreams.

Vivian wasn't listening. She was suddenly staring intently at Julie. "I'm sorry, what did you say your name was?"

"Alice!" Roman said. But at the same time, Julie answered truthfully: "Julie."

"Julie?" Vivian suddenly perked up. "As in Julie Fray?"

Julie looked at Roman, who was already answering for her. "No!" he said. "Julie Haberdashem!"

"Wait a minute," Vivian said, snapping to attention. "Oh, I see what's going on here!" The sweetness had disappeared from her voice. The circles under her eyes were back too.

"Nothing's going on!" Roman said quickly. "Nothing at all!"

Vivian ignored Roman. She glared right at Julie. "You're trying to steal my part! You little *witch*! You're even pretending to be 'in character'!"

"What?" Julie said meekly. "No, no, I'm Julie Haberdashem, just like he said. A temporary dreamstage worker."

Vivian took a step backward and waved at Julie's clothing. "If you're a dreamstage worker, how come you're dressed like that?"

Julie looked down at herself. "Like what?"

"You're in costume! *Pajamas?* That has to be for some future nightmare, right?" Vivian's nose flared in fury. "Don't tell me they've already fitted you for the part! Oh, we'll see about *that*!"

She whirled about to her makeup table and snatched up the receiver to the phone. "Operator?" she barked. "Give me Security!"

"No, really!" Julie said. "I don't want any part!"

Roman grabbed Julie by the hand. "Come on—let's get out of here."

"But—"

"*Now!*" he said, yanking her out the door.

)

ROMAN PULLED Julie down the alleys between the dream-stage warehouses. They passed more silent, faceless Moon People, some in golf carts, some carrying props and other supplies. None of the creatures seemed to take any notice of Julie and Roman. They reached a row of bungalows on the other side of the dream-studio lot, and that's when Roman finally stopped.

Julie was out of breath from running so hard. "Is Vivian always that . . . strange?" she asked Roman.

"It's the creative juices," he said. "From the creative juices tank? Vivian's addicted to the stuff. Everyone at the dream-studio used to get a share, but now Vivian gets almost all of it, which is funny because it sure hasn't made her very creative."

Julie had opened her mouth to ask another question when a strange roar suddenly blared out from the other side of the dream-studio. It sounded like a cross between a lion and an elephant.

Julie shivered. "What was *that*?"

"Vivian called Security," Roman said.

"What sort of security guards sound like *that*?"

"The Trull. They make sure nothing ever disrupts the dream-production."

"The Trull?" said Julie. "What *are* they?"

Roman ignored the question. "We've got to hide." He ducked toward the nearest bungalow. The window was dark. "Quick, in here."

Roman threw open the door and pushed Julie inside, following right behind. Then they crouched in the dark behind the door, listening.

Almost immediately a light flickered on behind them.

"Can I *help* you?" said a voice.

Julie and Roman spun around like they'd been caught in a searchlight. The inside of the bungalow was almost completely filled with stacks and stacks of screenplays. She'd seen such scripts in her dad's bungalow, but never this many. There must have been thousands of them, each bound with small brass brads, then piled haphazardly atop one another, and on top of an unlit cast-iron woodstove near the wall.

In the center of all those scripts was a small desk with a lamp and typewriter (and more scripts). A young man sat at the desk. He wasn't as handsome as Roman, but he had a pleasant face, with wire-rim glasses and a beard of dark stubble.

"Oh!" Roman said. "I didn't think there was anyone in here."

"S'okay," said the young man.

"What were you doing, sitting here in the dark?" Julie asked. She wasn't sure if it was rude, but she was curious.

"Thinking," he said. "I do some of my best thinking in the dark."

"What were you thinking about?"

"Dreams. After all, I *am* the dreamwriter."

"The what?" said Julie.

"The dreamwriter. You know, the person who writes the dreams?" He nodded around at the stacks of scripts. "These are my dreamplays." He frowned. "Don't tell me you didn't know that dreams have writers. What, did you think they just wrote themselves?"

"I never really thought about it," Julie admitted.

"Well, you *should!*" he said. "Because without writers, there wouldn't be any dreams at all. Say, who are you anyway? Wait, don't tell me!" He gazed at her, pressing his fingers to his temples like a fortune-teller doing a mind reading. Then he announced, "You're a stranger in a strange land on the run for a crime you didn't commit!"

"Huh?" Julie said. But when she thought about it, what the dreamwriter had said sort of made sense. "How did you know all that?"

"Hey, I'm a writer. We almost always know what's happened, and what's going to happen next. We know all the story lines."

"You really write the dreams?" Julie asked.

The dreamwriter shrugged smugly. "I do indeed."

That gave Julie an idea. Roman had said he didn't have any power over the direction of the dreams. And Vivian certainly wasn't going to be doing Julie any favors anytime soon. But the dreamwriter . . .

"Do you think you could stop writing all those nightmares?" Julie blurted.

The dreamwriter leaned back in his chair, lacing his fingers behind his head. "As a matter of fact, lately I've been thinking of going in an entirely different direction with the dreams."

"You *have*? Is it a *happy* direction?"

Suddenly something thumped loudly against the roof of the bungalow. "Ouch!" said a voice, echoing down through the metal stovepipe. Julie heard a clang, then a long scraping sound, like something was sliding down the pipe. "Oooooowwwww!" said the voice.

A metal bird burst out of the pipe and landed in a big puff of ashes at the bottom of the stove. It was the same creature Julie had seen earlier flying under the streetlamp, but now its graceful wings were drooped and askew.

The bird stayed flat on its back inside the woodstove. "Script pick-up," it said, sounding exhausted.

The voice of the bird was female. It was also muffled, as if it were coming from *inside* the bird's metal casing. The creature's metal beak wasn't moving either. *It isn't a robot*, Julie realized, *but rather a shell or armor of some sort with someone or something on the inside!*

"What *is* that?" she asked Roman.

"A knight-bird," he answered matter-of-factly.

"A night-bird? Because it flies around at night?"

"A *knight*-bird. With a *k*. Because it's made entirely of metal. There are lots of them around here. They're used as couriers."

"Excuse me," said the dreamwriter to Julie and Roman. "This'll just take a second."

The dreamwriter quickly crossed to the stove and opened the leather pouch attached to the knight-bird's stomach. He slid a thick stack of papers from the pouch and replaced it with a script from his desk.

"Okay, you've made your pick-up," said the dreamwriter to the bird. "Now go on, get out of here!"

But the knight-bird suddenly found the energy to sit upright in the ashes. "What's *this*?" said the bird. "You have *guests*? You weren't going to introduce me?"

"I'm Julie," said Julie. "And this is Roman."

"Greta," said the knight-bird.

"The dreamwriter was just telling us his plans to write happier dreams!" said Julie excitedly.

Greta turned to the dreamwriter. Her metal head squeaked like the tin woodsman in *The Wizard of Oz*. "What's this I hear?"

"Why not?" said the dreamwriter. "I'm the writer, aren't I?"

The knight-bird began to laugh, great booming cackles that echoed inside the tin.

"What's so funny?" Julie asked the knight-bird.

"The dreamwriter doesn't have any say on what goes into the dreams!" said Greta, still chortling. "He just writes what the dream-producer tells him to!"

"That's not *true!*" snapped the dreamwriter. But he was already flushing a deep shade of red.

"Who's the dream-producer?" Julie asked the bird.

"The producer of the dreams," Greta said. "He picks the scripts, hires the actors, controls the whole dream-studio."

"Well, the dreamwriter must have *some* say," Julie said.

"I *do!*" the dreamwriter piped up.

Greta shook her metal head. "Nope. I carry the dreamplays back and forth, and I know the dreamwriter doesn't write one word that the dream-producer doesn't tell him to write. You should see the set of notes that I just delivered from the dream-producer about the dreamwriter's last script. Harsh!"

"Is that true?" Julie asked the dreamwriter.

"Well," he said stiffly, "the dream-producer might offer a few suggestions here and there."

"A few *suggestions?*" mocked the bird.

Suddenly the dreamwriter began to wail. "Okay, it's true! I'm a hack, all right? But I don't have a choice—I signed a contract! And if I don't do everything the dream-producer tells me to do—"

Just outside the bungalow, one of the half-elephant/half-lion creatures bellowed again—a trumpetlike blast as if from some hellish marching band.

Everyone in that office blanched, including Julie.

"The Trull," said Roman. "They must have caught our scent. We can't stay here."

"Good thing there's a back door to this place!" said Greta.

Roman prodded Julie through the stacks of scripts to the door in the rear. "We've got to get you back to wherever you came from," he said, staying surprisingly calm.

Wherever I came from? thought Julie.

"You say you just found yourself at the top of the creative juices tank," Roman went on. "So somehow that must be your way back home. So we'll sneak around the Trull, and I can take you back to the creative juices tank, and—"

"No," Julie interrupted him.

He stared at her. "What?"

"I'm not going home yet. There's something I need to do first."

"What do you need to do?"

"Go see this dream-producer," she said. "Because I'm not leaving Slumberia until I stop my nightmares once and for all."

4

The Creative Desert

Julie wasn't exactly sure when she had decided for a fact that Slumberia was real—that this really *was* a place inside her own head where they "filmed" her dreams. Maybe it was what she had seen in Roman's soft brown eyes. Nothing in a dream had ever looked so real—and so expressive. Or maybe it was just the way Julie felt. She was somehow *awake*—more awake than she had been in ages. In a way, Julie had known this was more than a dream right from the start.

In any event, she *had* decided it was real. This place, Slumberia, really was the source of all her dreams—and her nightmares. And that meant she had a chance to stop those nightmares once and for all.

So now she didn't *want* to go back home. Not yet.

"Julie," said Roman, who was still standing by the back door of the dreamwriter's bungalow, "you can't stay here. You saw how Vivian reacted. And what about the Trull? If they catch you—"

"You don't understand!" Julie exclaimed. "I *have* to stop my nightmares. If I don't, if I have to live with them for even one more day, I'll go crazy!"

Roman stared at her. Julie wasn't sure he understood what she had said—that he had any notion that what they filmed in this dream-studio were *her* nightmares, and that she had to live through each and every horrible one.

But Julie saw in the gentle depths of his eyes that somehow he *did* understand—that, if nothing else, he knew exactly how important this was to her.

He nodded. "All right. I'll take you to Castle Alucard."

"Castle Alucard?"

"The home of the dream-producer."

Julie was confused. "He's not here in the dream-studio?"

"No," Roman said, his voice dropping. "He's definitely not here in the dream-studio."

)

AT THE same time, in another part of the dream-studio, Vivian Clavier stood in the doorway of her trailer, smiling at the sounds of the savage Trull.

"Just wait," she muttered to herself. "When the Trull are finished with them, they'll wish they'd never fooled with Vivian Clavier. Off with their heads!"

She glanced in the direction of the creative juices tank.

Her eyes caught something suspended in the air just above the top of the tank—a big black spot.

How strange, thought Vivian.

Her first impulse was to call the Trull, but something held her tongue. Nothing unusual ever happened in the dreamstudio; now two unusual things had happened in one night. First that strange girl had tried to steal her part, now this strange dark spot.

Can it be that these two events are connected? Vivian wondered.

She decided to check the black spot out for herself. She started toward the creative juices tank, walking faster and faster with each step. When she reached the base of the metal ladder, she skittered, insectlike, up to the top. She felt like an idiot out there in the cold, but her gut told her that whatever she had seen hanging above this tower was somehow important.

The metal tank was curved at the top. Vivian had to find her balance. She looked up at the black spot.

It floated in the air. It was moving—roiling and throbbing vaguely—but making no noise. It looked so *black,* like liquid darkness.

It reminded Vivian of a hole. *But in the air? Where would that lead?*

It was the most amazing thing Vivian had ever seen. Was this a prop or set piece for some nightmare? Vivian hadn't read any scripts that included anything like this. And how would they get it to hang in the air like that? Besides, what would a prop be doing here at the top of the creative juices tank?

But if it wasn't something for a nightmare scene, what was it?

Vivian stepped closer, until she was right underneath it. Oddly, she wasn't frightened. On the contrary, she was fascinated.

She would have to stand on her tiptoes to touch it, but she could if she wanted to.

Even now Vivian wasn't the least bit uneasy. She knew this hole was somehow a very big deal—the answer to a long-unsolved mystery.

Vivian reached up toward the spot. It gurgled

The second she touched it, it began to suck at her. Vivian started in surprise, but she didn't pull her hand away. Instead, she let it draw her up.

It pulled her inside, slowly at first—arm, then head, then shoulders.

Before she knew it, it quickly sucked the rest of Vivian Clavier up inside like a milkshake through a plastic straw.

)

ROMAN FOUND some shoes and a coat for Julie in a closet in the dreamwriter's bungalow, and quickly ushered her out the back door, then through an unlocked door in the concrete wall that surrounded the dream-studio.

There were no lights outside that wall except for the weak glow of the moon. The land was hilly and uneven, but no grass or trees or plants grew on the Slumberian countryside; only rocks covered the landscape. The air was just as still and stale as it had seemed inside the studio walls. It smelled like an old sponge.

Julie did a double-take at the moon, which was almost full. "That's funny," she said to herself. "I could have sworn there was just a half-moon before."

Roman nodded her on. "We should hurry."

For a long time, they jogged without speaking. Julie was still a little unsettled by the idea that they were being chased by monsters of some sort. But she was mostly excited by the fact that she had been given a chance to finally put a stop to her nightmares.

When they stopped for a moment, Roman listened for the roar of the Trull, to know if they'd been followed. But the sound of pursuit did not come, and Roman seemed to breathe a sigh of relief.

He turned and pointed into the distance.

"There," he said. "That's Castle Alucard."

The silhouette of a massive castle on a hill stood out against the moonlit sky. It looked tall and blocky, a towering assortment of crude rectangles. It also looked dark and ominous, especially under the looming moon.

"Oh," Julie said, suddenly feeling a lot less excited. "Well, at least it won't be long before sunrise." Julie wondered what would happen then. No doubt she'd wake up back in the "real" world, and this whole weird behind-the-scenes-of-a-dream would come to an end. That just made it more important that they get to the dream-producer quickly, so she could convince him to make happier dreams.

But to Julie's surprise, Roman frowned. "Sunrise?"

"You know," Julie said. "Sunrise. When the sun comes up. Morning." He kept looking at her blankly, so she added, "The *sun*? The big round thing up in the sky? Like the moon, only brighter?"

"Oh, right, like in the dreams. No, we don't have a 'sunrise' in Slumberia, not anymore."

"No sun? No daylight?"

"Nope."

They started for the castle. The pebbles and stones of the Slumberian countryside crunched under their feet.

"Well, if there's no sun," Julie said, "what's *that*?"

She had spotted a glowing light on the horizon.

)

IT WASN'T the sun. It was a white lighthouse with a brightly gleaming beacon on top.

It had been built on rock at the edge of an immense basin of milky white sand. Julie and Roman climbed up next to the lighthouse and stared out over the moonlit panorama. The sand began right below their feet.

"The Creative Desert," Roman said, his voice fading into the expanse.

"It's so *empty*," Julie said, describing not just the vast desert, but also the way it made her feel inside. The sand was absolutely smooth and utterly lifeless. It looked like it had never even been touched.

Roman took a step back from the edge. "Let's push on," he said. "Something about this place doesn't feel right."

But Julie wanted very much to touch that sand. It beckoned to her like a field of freshly fallen snow.

Roman faced the lighthouse. "I wonder why there's a lighthouse here."

Fascinated, Julie sat on her heels. She reached out to touch the pristine sand.

"*Stop!*" shouted a voice from the top of the lighthouse. "*Get away from there!*"

Roman looked up, startled. "Huh?"

"That sand!" bellowed the voice from the lighthouse. "Can't you see what's right in front of you?"

At that instant, Julie's fingers touched the sand. The sand was very fine, but also icy cold—so cold it burned.

"Ouch!" she said.

She snatched back her hand and glanced up over the desert. Only this time she didn't see a barren expanse in front of her. This time, she saw people.

Not people.

Ghosts!

Where had they come from? Julie wasn't sure. It was as if they had just appeared. Or maybe they'd been there all along, invisible and then suddenly winking into view.

There were dozens of them crowding the sand in front of Julie, reaching out for her, desperate to make contact. They were vague, ashen beings rippling in some otherworldly breeze. Their features blurred in and out of focus, never quite forming completely. They made no noise.

Julie screamed and jerked back from the sand. But she wasn't fast enough, and one of the ghostly hands gripped her by the shoulder.

It felt like she was being stabbed by an icicle; the touch of the ghost was that cold. The chill penetrated deeply, into her arm, neck, and chest—and headed straight for her heart. Suddenly she couldn't breathe.

She tried to pull away, but the grip of the ghost was too strong. And it wasn't just cold; it was also sucking the warmth right from her body. Even as Julie felt the life draining from her, she saw the ghost growing stronger, already glowing more brightly, looking more focused. The face was still blurry, but an excited smile formed on its silent, cruel lips.

A second ghostly hand grabbed her. Julie hadn't thought she could get any colder, but she did. She hadn't thought there was any more warmth to be drawn from her body either, but there was. The second ghost began to glow brighter too.

More spectral hands clawed and clutched at Julie. She was so cold she could no longer move. The ghosts had her, and they were pulling her frozen body down with them into the white, untouched sand.

)

VIVIAN CLAVIER jerked upright in bed, as if from a bad dream. She was in the bedroom of a young girl. There was a wardrobe, a picture window, and an antique looking-glass that hung over the dresser.

It looked like the Julie Fray bedroom set from the dream-studio. But it *wasn't* a set. There were four walls, not three, and there were no cameras or lights. So where *was* she? And how had she arrived here?

The last thing Vivian remembered was climbing to the top of the creative juices tank, and then investigating some strange phenomenon in the air. She had touched it, and it had somehow sucked her inside.

And she had ended up here, in this strange place.

Vivian slipped out of bed. She was wearing the pajamas that that strange girl at the dream-studio had been wearing—the actress who had been trying to steal her part.

"Stupid cow!" she fumed.

She glanced around the room, searching for something that would help all this make sense. Vivian was nothing if not shrewd; she knew she'd figure this out eventually.

On the dresser, she spied a book—a journal. She walked closer.

Julie's Diary, read the words on the cover.

"Aha!" Vivian said, grinning happily.

She snatched up the diary and sat back down on the bed. Then she opened it up and began to read.

)

ROMAN SLAMMED against Julie with all his might, knocking her away from the frozen grip of the desert ghosts.

The phantoms kept clawing for her, so he yanked her back from the desert's edge. The ghosts were apparently unable to leave the sand itself, because they did not follow.

"Are you okay?" Roman asked Julie, deep concern in his voice and eyes.

She shivered, cold to the core of her being. But as quickly as the cold had seized her, warmth was already flowing back into her body again.

"She'll be fine!" came the voice from the top of the light-house. "They can't get you if they can't touch you. And they can't touch you if you stay away from the sand!"

Julie pushed herself upright, gaping at the ghosts still gathered at the edge of the desert. They weren't reaching for her anymore. But they were still gazing at her longingly, clutching their own blurry faces and moaning in silent despair. The sight sickened her. The whole experience had left her very shaken.

"Thanks," Roman said to the person at the top of the lighthouse. "Whoever you are."

Julie turned toward the lighthouse. The light at the top had since gone out. Someone was climbing down a cable along the face of the tower.

Julie forced herself to stand. "I'm Julie," she said haltingly. "And we're on our way to—"

She froze. Suspended from the side of the lighthouse was something long and white and snakelike.

"Roman?" said Julie, taken aback. "What's *that*?"

"What do you mean?" he answered. "It's the glowworm from the top of the lighthouse."

Glowworm? thought Julie.

But Roman was right: it was a worm, not a snake, and it was sliding down on some white cable or rope. The creature was at least five feet long, as thick as a tire, and hanging in a giant spiral.

The worm touched the ground at last. The "rope" it was using for its descent came out of the tail end of the creature itself. *It's silk,* Julie realized. *The creature is a giant silkworm!*

The worm wiggled over toward them.

"That wasn't so smart, trying to touch that sand," the worm said. She had a sweet voice, full of honesty and openness, like that of a friendly young waitress in some small-town diner.

"I . . ." Julie said. "I didn't know!"

"That's the Creative Desert. You don't know what that means?"

Julie shook her head.

"Desert ghosts!"

Julie looked back at the desert. By now most of the ghosts had disappeared again. A few still remained vaguely visible, looking aimless and glum. But even they were quickly fading away.

"What *are* they?" Julie said.

The worm sighed. "What is any ghost? Faded memories. Spirits that refuse to die. Things so dead and tired that the only way they can survive at all is to come here to the Creative Desert."

"Why here?" asked Roman.

"Because this used to be the Lake of Creativity. It was a whole lake full of creative juices! Used to be ships and everything sailing up from the Sea of Emotion. It's all dried up now, but there's a little bit of residue from all that creative juice in there still. That's what them ghosts live on. There's just enough left to keep 'em from fading away completely. It takes the presence of someone with some essence, someone like you"—she nodded at Julie—"to make them fully visible. But even that ain't enough to keep 'em visible for long."

Julie shivered one more time, wondering if she'd ever feel completely warm again. "What would've happened if they'd pulled me into the sand with them?"

"Oh, now," said the worm, "no point in dwelling on the negative, is there? Name's Meg."

"Roman."

"Julie." She hesitated. "I don't mean to be rude, but if the lake's all dried up, how come you still keep the lighthouse lit? There can't be any more ships."

Meg shook her head sadly. "No, there ain't no more ships. But I don't have much choice now, do I? A contract's a contract, and my contract says I gotta stay here and light this lighthouse, whether there are any ships here or not. Anyway, a job's a job. Ain't that many things a glowworm can do, to tell you the truth."

"But you're also a silkworm," Julie pointed out.

"Well, now, that is very true! Every glowworm's a silkworm. Of course, not every silkworm can glow. Seems kinda unfair, but what can you do? Say, where you folks headed?"

"We're off to see the dream-producer," Roman said.

"Oh! I can see his castle from atop my lighthouse. Ain't never been there myself." The glowworm sighed. "I ain't never been nowhere. And I always did so want to travel."

"So why don't you?" Julie said.

"Well, it's my contract. Don't allow no vacation days."

"The dreamwriter was under contract too," said Julie, thinking out loud.

"Dreamwriter?" said the glowworm.

"The person who writes the dreams that they film back in the dream-studio."

"Someone *writes* them dreams?"

"I know," Julie said. "Who knew?"

A familiar roar boomed out into the night—fingernails down the blackboard of Julie's soul.

"The Trull!" Roman said. "They followed us!"

And it sounded like they were very, very close.

5

Of Moats and Mirrors

VIVIAN PEEKED inside the kitchen at Julie's house and saw two people: a woman who looked exactly like the actress who played Julie's mother in the dreams, and a man who looked exactly like the actor who played Julie's father.

Vivian didn't miss a beat. She sashayed into the kitchen and spoke in what may have been her sweetest voice ever. "Mom! Dad! Good *morning!*"

Julie's mother looked up from where she was working at the counter. "Julie!" she said.

Julie's father looked up from his newspaper. "Well, good morning, Julie!" he said.

It's working! thought Vivian. These two old people really did think she was Julie. But that made sense, since Vivian had played this character—to perfection!—in so many nightmares. But this wasn't a Julie who was torn between her parents. This was a Julie who was going to be getting exactly what she wanted from them both. Now Vivian just had to figure out what that was.

Julie's mother held up a tray. "Would you like a blueberry muffin? The key is a dash of real lemon juice. And fresh blueberries, of course."

Vivian took a muffin. "Wow, they look *great*."

"Taste great too," muttered Julie's dad. "At least if you like your muffins burned on the outside."

Ah! thought Vivian. Julie's parents were testing her, trying to make her take sides between them. It was exactly what she'd read all about in the bedroom in that book called *Julie's Diary*. It was just like in the dreams too. If she said she *liked* the muffin, Julie's mother won. If she *didn't* like it, Julie's father won.

Julie's parents both looked at her expectantly.

"Oh, I'm going to save my muffin for the trip to school," Vivian said. "I should be going anyway. Now, this 'bus' thing—where do I catch that again?"

Julie's mother turned away, annoyed. "At the bus stop just up the street, of course."

Vivian thumped herself on the head. "Of course! How could I have forgotten that?"

But as she was leaving the kitchen, Julie's father spoke up. "I'll see you tonight at the studio, right?"

Vivian perked up. Studio? She liked the sound of that word a lot.

)

"*Run,*" Roman said to Julie back at the edge of the Creative Desert. "Maybe we can outrun the Trull."

He and Julie turned and bolted straight for Castle Alucard, which was just over a nearby hill.

"Wait for me!" Meg said, furiously wiggling after them. "I sure don't want to be here when the Trull arrive!"

A few minutes later, when they reached the base of the castle, Julie was sweaty and out of breath. Somehow they had evaded the Trull. Better still, the running had finally countered the last of the chill of the desert ghosts.

Castle Alucard was a fortress of rock and iron. Almost everything about it was oversized: the massive blocks of stone that formed its walls, the wide soaring towers. And everything else about it—the moat, the raised drawbridge, the sharp iron spikes that jutted up from the top of the battlements—said, *Stay away!* Indeed, the fin of a shark suddenly burst up out of the water in the moat. A second fin popped up several yards away. The moat was thick with algae, but it bubbled and churned from the motion of circling sharks.

"Not exactly welcoming, is it?" Meg said.

Just then, the drawbridge began to squeak. The chains holding it upright rattled as the bridge was slowly lowered across the moat. At the same time, a pair of massive wooden double doors on the other side of the drawbridge creaked inward.

"I guess someone is expecting us," said Roman.

"Maybe," said Meg, "but talk about your mixed messages!"

Julie turned to the glowworm. "You don't need to come inside with us, you know."

"And miss seeing the castle?" said Meg. "That's crazy talk! Didn't I say I always wanted to travel?"

Julie faced the castle, spine stiffened. Whatever was in that castle, it couldn't be as bad as her nightmares. And in order to stop them, she needed to go inside.

She started forward. Just then, something sleek and gray lurched up out of the water. Julie gasped.

"Help!" said the gray thing flailing in the moat. "Shark attack! Help!"

Julie gaped. It wasn't a shark: it was a drowning young man!

She hurried to the edge of the moat and reached out to the man. "Help me get him up!" Julie said to Roman.

"Julie," Roman said, hesitating, "are you *sure?*"

"Of course I'm sure! Quick, before the sharks get him!"

Together, she and Roman started hauling the struggling young man onto dry land. His gray suit was all in tatters.

But he was only halfway out of the water when Julie saw a gray dorsal fin poking up directly behind him.

"Shark!" Julie said to Roman, as she pulled desperately at the man. "Hurry!"

Julie and Roman dragged him the rest of the way out of

the water, and he collapsed in an exhausted heap. In one hand he clutched a bruised leather briefcase.

"You were being attacked by sharks, and yet you held on to your briefcase?" Julie asked in surprise.

"Well, of course!" said the young man, breathing heavily. "Without my legal pads, I would have been completely defenseless."

Julie gasped again. It wasn't a man at all! Oh, yes, he had arms and legs like a man, but he also had pale gray skin and a long narrow head that rose up to a dull peak. Several inches below his chin were two sets of fleshy slits, like gills, one on each side of his Adam's apple.

"Allow me to introduce myself," said the creature, standing and straightening the lapels of his shredded suit. "The name's Bentley J. Montbank, attorney-at-law." His mouth was full of rows of sharp yellow teeth, and a pointed dorsal fin stuck out through a slit in the back of his jacket.

She'd thought he was being attacked by a shark; the truth was, he *was* a shark!

"My card?" said the creature, pulling a soggy white business card from his suit. He even had webbing between his fingers.

"You're a *shark*?" said Julie, still not quite able to accept the obvious.

"Yes, and boy, am I glad you came along when you did! The other sharks were eating me alive down there."

"But . . . ?"

"So! What brings you to Castle Alucard?"

Julie glanced at Roman. "Uh, we want to see the dream-producer, so I can—"

"Ah!" Bentley said. "So you can *sue* him! *Now* you're talking! It won't be easy—unfortunately, the dream-producer has very few liquid assets. Just the moat, to tell you the truth. But we can do it! The dreams he's producing just aren't safe. They don't even have seat belts!"

"No, no!" Julie said. "I don't want to *sue* the dream-producer. I just want to talk to him."

"Oh," he said, his face falling. "Well. Are you sure?"

"I'm just trying to stop the dream-studio from producing more nightmares," Julie explained. "I met the dreamwriter, and he said—"

"Dreams have writers?"

"I know. Weird, huh?"

"Well, you'd be foolish to see the dream-producer without a lawyer at hand." The shark bent down and clicked open his briefcase. "And as a matter of fact, I happen to specialize in dream-law."

"Really?" Julie said. "I don't have any money, but—"

Bentley snapped his briefcase closed like a bear spring-trap. "It's been so nice chatting with you!"

"Come on, Julie," Roman said, pulling her arm. "We're wasting time."

Bentley sighed. "Wait," he muttered. "I might as well go with you. I'll work pro bono. That means free. I don't care if I *did* sign a contract."

Yet another contract? thought Julie.

Julie looked at Roman. "Well?"

He shrugged. "I guess it couldn't hurt to have a lawyer."

)

JUST BEYOND the front door of the castle was a narrow foyer with wood paneling on the walls and red carpet on the floor. Candles flickered in sconces on either side of the room, but the far wall was dark. It smelled of dust and decay.

"Hello?" Roman called into the darkness. "Mr. Dream-Producer?"

The door slammed shut behind them.

"That ain't good," Meg mumbled.

Flames flared up, as if by magic, in candle sconces farther down the hall. It wasn't a foyer, but a corridor—one that seemed to include no doors.

"Someone wants us to go this way," Roman said.

Julie and her friends walked (and wiggled) deeper into the castle. As soon as they passed by a candle, it fizzled out, its light replaced by a flame flickering up in another sconce just down the hall. That meant the corridor was always dark behind and ahead of them—everywhere except in the exact place where they were.

Soon the corridor turned.

And turned again.

They passed faded tapestries and paintings, and dusty

suits of armor, and mounted swords covered with cobwebs.

The hallway kept turning this way and that, sometimes rising up small flights of stairs. But there were still no exits.

Finally, the last of the candle sconces fizzled out. Julie and her friends had entered a large room. Moonlight from a big picture window spilled across the floor.

It was a parlor. Plush velvet couches and a divan with tasseled cushions surrounded a big stone fireplace, currently unlit. Tabletop vases held brittle arrangements of dried flowers and frayed peacock feathers. A large antique globe hung at an angle on a wooden stand. As with the corridor, it was all very dusty, like it had been sitting untouched and unmoved for a very long time. And it smelled of heavy incense, as if from a funeral.

"Hello?" Roman said again. "Mr. Dream-Producer?"

Julie caught her breath. Someone was facing them on the other side of the parlor—someone familiar.

Vivian!

No, Julie thought. It wasn't Vivian; this time, it really *was* Julie. It was her own reflection in a large mirror hanging on the opposite wall. It was exactly the same size as the picture window, with the same frame and same thick velvet curtains, pulled open.

"That's odd," said Meg. "Curtains on a mirror?"

Suddenly the reflection in the mirror began to fade. It was being replaced by a different image.

"Something's happening," Roman said.

They walked (and wiggled) closer. In the center of the room, they stopped.

The image in the mirror was of Julie in her class at school. Recess had just started, but she had stayed behind to talk to her teacher.

"Ms. Ely?" said the image of Julie. "Can I talk to you a minute?"

"Yes, Julie?" said Ms. Ely.

So the image even had sound. It was like a television screen, but somehow seemed far more real.

Julie suddenly understood why the mirror had curtains. It *was* a window, but a different kind of one. She was looking *through* the mirror—to another place entirely.

"I just wanted to tell you how much I enjoyed today's class," the image of Julie was saying. "You had me hanging on your every word! I had no idea math could be so *exciting*."

"Really?" said Ms. Ely, obviously flattered. "Well, thank you very much, Julie. That's nice of you to say."

Julie couldn't remember ever complimenting her teacher like that. On the contrary, Julie always seemed to be saying the wrong thing to Ms. Ely. She wondered if this was the future she was seeing in the mirror.

"I can hardly wait to see what you do with history!" said Julie-in-the-mirror with a musical laugh.

"I don't laugh like that," Julie said, frowning. And that's

how she knew the girl in the mirror wasn't her. It looked a lot like her. But this girl had more confidence—more presence. Julie could hardly take her eyes off her.

"That's not me," Julie told her friends.

"Then who is it?" Roman asked.

He and Julie looked at each other.

"Vivian!" they said at exactly the same time.

At that instant, the mirror went dark. A second later, it was back to being a normal mirror again.

"I don't understand what that was," Julie said. "What was Vivian doing in my class at school?"

"I don't know," Roman said. But he looked worried.

There was movement in the parlor of the dream-producer, a shadow across the moon.

"Vivian is there," said a man with a soft, beguiling voice, "because she's taken your place back in your world!"

6

The Producer's Ploy

WHO *SAID* that?" Julie said, turning around in the darkened parlor.

"*I* did."

A man stood in silhouette against the picture window. But as hard as Julie stared, she couldn't make out anything about the figure, except that he was tall and dressed all in black.

"It's so dark in here," Julie said. "Is there a light?"

"I like the dark," said the man.

The drapes swayed in a draft that Julie never felt.

"Are you the dream-producer?" Roman asked.

"That's right," said the man. "Ethan Alucard." But the figure was gone from the window. The voice was now coming from the opposite side of the room. Julie turned. The dream-producer had somehow moved to the parlor's tabletop bar. "May I offer you something to drink?" he asked. "Creative juice? Bottled water?"

"No, thank you," Julie said, wondering how she'd missed seeing him cross the room.

"What did you mean about Vivian taking Julie's place?" Roman asked.

"Well, now, that's quite complicated," Alucard said. "But Julie can explain it. Can't you, Julie?"

"How do you know my name?" Julie said.

"Oh, I know everything about you, Julie." He had magically moved again. When he spoke, he was directly behind them now, not five feet away. "After all," whispered the dream-producer, "I produce *your* dreams, don't I?"

Julie spun about to face him. How was it that he was able to move across the room so quickly, and without her seeing? Was he a man or a shadow? After all, even now she still couldn't make out his face.

"So it's true!" said Julie. "All of this—the dream-studio, Slumberia—it's all real, and it's all inside my head?"

"That's right," he said. "Slumberia is the place inside your brain where your dreams come from. That's the source of the creative juice—your brain."

"But that means this whole land is only as old as I am—eleven years?"

"Oh, we're much older than that."

"But—"

"Who's to say you didn't exist even before you were born?" Alucard said. "In some form or another."

How was it, Julie wondered, that the dream-producer

knew all this? No one before now—not Roman, not even the dreamwriter—had seemed to be aware of the existence of the "real" world.

"How did I get here?" Julie asked.

"Humans have one brain, but two minds," Alucard explained. "The waking mind and the sleeping mind. The conscious and the unconscious. The waking mind is the part you're aware of—your day-to-day thoughts and the voice inside your head. The sleeping mind is everything else—everything you're *not* aware of, your dreams and memories and emotions. Slumberia is one part of your sleeping mind."

He paused. "But something has gone wrong. Earlier tonight, a breach opened in the wall between your waking and sleeping minds. And so, while you were sleeping, your waking mind slipped over into Slumberia."

"That black spot in the air over the creative juices tank!" Julie exclaimed. "Is that what that was? Was that the breach in the wall between my waking and sleeping minds?"

"Yesss," Alucard said.

"Is this making any sense to you?" Roman asked Meg.

"Not the slightest bit," said the worm.

Julie looked for the dream-producer, but he had shifted again. She didn't know where he was now. "So you really *can* stop my nightmares?" she said to the room itself.

"Perhapsss." Alucard stood near the doorway. "But Julie, aren't you worried about getting home?"

"Home?" said Julie. "What do you mean? Won't I just wake up when morning comes?"

"Morning *came*, Julie. Hours ago. You woke up right as usual. You're at school now. You saw it yourself just a moment ago in the Mirror of the Minds."

"That was *real*?"

"Of course."

"But how is that possible? I thought my waking mind was here in Slumberia. How could I be at school if my mind is here?" Up until now Julie had thought she understood everything the dream-producer was saying. But suddenly she was all confused again.

"*Vivian*," Alucard whispered. He was now standing next to the darkened mirror.

"That actress who plays me in my dreams?" said Julie. "What about her?"

"She crawled through the breach in the wall between your waking and sleeping minds. Then she took over. She became your waking mind. She became *you*."

Julie still didn't understand. Vivian had *become* her?

With a wave of his hand, Alucard brought the mirror on the wall to life again. But even as the mirror brightened, the dream-producer himself seemed to stay a shadow.

The picture in the mirror was still that of Julie—or, rather, Vivian!—back at school. But now she was out on the playground with the other kids.

Vivian was talking to Veronica Sutton and Ashley Gold, the two most popular girls in class.

"Oh, no," Vivian was saying, "you should only use liquid eyeliner on the upper lashes. Always use a pencil for the lower ones."

"Really?" Ashley said.

Vivian nodded. "And if you want a more dramatic look, use a color pencil for the lower lashes. But dot, don't draw."

Veronica and Ashley had always used to laugh at Julie. But now they were hanging on Vivian's every word. Meanwhile, Julie could see her best friend, Lisa Pituro, lurking in the background, obviously confused by Vivian's behavior.

"What are you *doing*?" Julie spoke to the mirror. "Don't talk to Veronica and Ashley! Can't you see how phony they are? And don't ignore Lisa like that! What must she think of me?"

"She can't hear you, Julie," Alucard said. The mirror flickered, then faded again. "There is no contact between the waking and sleeping minds. Just the dreams themselves. And this mirror, of course. Information comes in through the Mirror of the Minds. And it goes out through the dreams."

"But what about the breach in the wall between her waking and sleeping minds?" said Roman. "Can't Julie get back home through that?" Julie was impressed that he'd picked up on things so quickly.

"Yes, the breach," said the dream-producer matter-of-factly.

"Unfortunately, that won't stay open for long. It's healing, you see. And by moonset tonight, it will be healed completely."

"What does *that* mean?" asked Roman.

"It means that Vivian would continue to control Julie's waking mind," said Alucard. "And that Julie would be stranded here in Slumberia."

"For how long?" said Meg.

"Well, the breach only opened because of the strain in Julie's waking mind. With Vivian in charge now, there is no more strain. So Julie would be stuck here . . . forever."

"Moonset?" said Julie. "What's that?" But Alucard had disappeared yet again.

"The moon works differently here in Slumberia," he said, suddenly standing at the picture window. "Back in your world, Julie, it takes about a month for the moon to go through its cycle, correct?"

"Yes," Julie said.

"But here in Slumberia, it only takes a single day. When you wake up in the morning in the 'real' world, the moon here in Slumberia is full. But as you go through the day, and as you become more and more tired, the Slumberian moon wanes, to a half-moon, then a quarter-moon. By the time it disappears completely, you're exhausted. And as you sleep, the moon grows larger and larger, until it's a full moon again and you're completely refreshed. Then in the 'real' world you wake up, and here in Slumberia we start the whole process all over again."

"Well, when will it be moonset?" Julie asked.

"Tonight," Roman said quietly. "When it's time for Vivian to go to sleep."

Julie looked out the picture window. The moon wasn't full anymore. In fact, it was already down to almost three-quarters. Now that the cycles of the Slumberian moon had been explained to her, Julie could actually see it slowly shrinking smaller and smaller.

"But that still gives me plenty of time to get back to the dream-studio!" Julie said. "Hours and hours."

"I suppose it does," said Alucard, shifting across the room to the unlit fireplace. He ran his fingers gently across the mantel.

Roman turned on him. "See here," he said. "How are you *doing* that?"

"Doing what?" he asked, like he really had no idea what Roman was talking about.

Suddenly Julie realized that she couldn't go back to the dream-studio yet—not until she got the dream-producer to agree to stop making nightmares.

"Please," Julie said. "What I said before about stopping the nightmares. Do you think you will?"

"Yessss," whispered the dream-producer. "But in exchange, you must first do something for me."

" 'Do something'?" Roman said suspiciously. "What does Julie have to *do*?"

"Tell me her dream," he said.

"What dream?" said Julie, confused again.

"Your deepest, most personal dream! The one thing you wish for more than anything else in the world. Tell me that, and I'll stop the nightmares."

"I want my parents to stop fighting, of course," Julie said. "To stop putting me in the middle, and to love each other again. Don't you know this already? I thought you watched me through the Mirror of the Minds."

"But I want to hear it in *your* words," said Alucard.

Julie whirled around, bumping against the large globe. It spun on its wooden axis. She'd been certain that the dream-producer had been right behind her again. But he wasn't there now. And how was it, Julie wondered, that in all this time, her eyes still hadn't adjusted to the dark?

"Why do you want to know my dreams and wishes anyway?" she asked pointedly.

When the dream-producer spoke, it was like he was all around them, speaking from everywhere at once. "Because that's what a producer *does*! I make wishes come true!"

"You mean," said Julie, "if I tell you a dream, you'll produce it in the dream-studio?"

"Oh, yes!" he said eagerly. "And I'll never produce another nightmare again!"

"Careful, Julie," warned Roman. "I think it's a trick!"

Bentley's briefcase clicked open. "We could always get that in writing."

"No," Julie said. "It's okay." She had figured it was a trick too. Alucard was up to something. If he wasn't, he would have shown himself by now. On the other hand, what choice did Julie have? She desperately wanted her night-mares stopped, and the dream-producer was the one person who could actually do that. And telling him her dream seemed harmless enough.

She began recounting the dream. "Well, I guess it would be Christmas morning, right before we open our presents. There'd be eggnog and cinnamon rolls and a big box of Christ-mas oranges. And my parents and I would be together, but they wouldn't be angry at each other. They'd still be in love."

"Yesssssss," whispered the dream-producer. She could feel his breath on the back of her neck, soft, but oddly cold. It tickled.

Julie thought about moving away, but she suddenly felt very tired, like she'd just sprinted up a flight of stairs.

"And then the doorbell rings," Julie went on, "and it's all my friends. . . ."

"Mmmmmmmm," moaned the dream-producer.

Julie felt dizzy now, and still so very, very tired. The breath on her neck had become a gentle slurping just under her right ear.

"Julie?" It was Roman's voice. It sounded far away. "Are you all right?"

"No," Julie said. "I feel strange. Sleepy." Her neck throbbed.

"Where are you?" Roman demanded.

"I'm here," she whispered. But suddenly the shadows in the parlor where thicker than ever. She could barely make out the furniture anymore. She couldn't see Roman, even though he had been standing right next to her.

"How did it get so dark?" Roman said. "*Julie? Where did you go? Say something.*"

But Julie was too tired to speak. She had never felt so exhausted in her whole life. She felt like a snowman as it melts. She would have fallen over, but something—or someone—was holding her up. Now there was something cold and wet on her neck.

"Julie!" Meg said. "Speak up!"

"Where *is* she?" Roman said to the dream-producer. "Where is Julie? I want you to turn on the lights!"

The dream-producer laughed—an evil cackle. "Lights? Oh, but there *are* no lights here!"

The darkness was now complete. Even the moon had faded to black. Julie hadn't seen anyone draw the curtains in front of the window. And yet the shadows had closed around her, like the ocean tide coming in around a beached ship. The slurping sound was louder now, also like the tide, but not an incoming one. It was more like an outgoing one.

But Roman said, "No lights, huh? Meg, we need light!"

"What's that?" said Meg.

"Turn on your glow-light!"

"Oh, *right!*"

The tail end of the worm's plump white body immediately began to glow.

"Wait!" said the dream-producer. "*Stop!*"

Meg's tail grew brighter still. Its light vanquished even the shadows of this dark and dreary parlor. Julie saw the dream-producer clearly at last. He was crouched down next to her, his head at her neck, but she still couldn't see his face.

"There he is!" Roman shouted. "Get away from her!"

With a snarl, the dream-producer looked up. "*No!*" he barked. "She's *mine!*"

His skin was pasty white, and his eyes glowed a vivid red. He had no reflection in the Mirror of the Minds.

A vampire!

Julie reached up and felt her neck, but there were no bite marks. He must have been draining something other than blood—something deeper, closer to her very essence. Like the ghosts on the Creative Desert, he'd been sucking at her very soul. Somehow he'd needed Julie's telling him her dream to get the flow started. No wonder she'd suddenly grown so tired!

"Get away from her," Roman said, calm, but commanding.

"Shut it off!" said the vampire, cowering from the light of the worm.

But Meg did not douse her light.

"Are you really the dream-producer?" Roman said.

The vampire nodded meekly, even as he shielded his stark white face with his cape.

"Can you really stop the nightmares?"

"No," he whimpered. "All my orders come via knight-bird from the dream-executives in Nightmare City. They're the ones with all the power."

"I knew it," Roman said. "He was lying all along."

Suddenly Alucard lunged for Roman.

"Roman!" Julie shouted.

Roman snatched up the object nearest to him in order to fend off the creature. Unfortunately, it was the globe.

"Great," he said dismally. "Just great."

Alucard flew at him.

Roman shielded himself with the globe. It collapsed under the force of the vampire's assault.

Alucard froze. Julie watched his face. His red eyes widened. Suddenly he fell limp. He'd impaled himself on the wooden stick—the wooden *stake*—that acted as the globe's axis.

The vampire crumbled to ash right in Roman's arms.

"Are you okay?" Roman asked Julie, even as he coolly brushed vampire ashes off himself.

"I'm fine," she said. She was shaken, but not as badly as she had been with the ghosts. It took more than vampires to truly scare her now. And her strength was already returning.

She picked up a vase off a nearby end table and threw it right at the Mirror of the Minds.

The mirror shattered, pieces cascading down onto the floor. The empty frame stayed hanging on the wall.

Roman bent down and picked up a piece of the broken mirror. He looked over at Julie, as if for an explanation.

"I really don't like the idea of people watching me without my permission," she said simply.

Suddenly a chorus of ferocious roars resounded out of the open doorway behind them.

The Trull! Julie and her friends hadn't outrun them after all.

7

The Labyrinth of Echoes

VIVIAN CLAVIER was having a perfectly marvelous day. It had taken all of three hours to become the most popular girl at Julie's school (not to mention ditch that worthless Lisa Pituro, *and* become the teacher's pet!).

But there had been no real challenge in that, so she'd left school during lunch. Vivian had hailed a taxi, something she had done in the dreams, and taken it to the television studio where Julie's father worked. The security guard at the front gate had, of course, mistaken her for Julie and let her inside. Now she was wandering around among the sets and sound-stages on the studio lot—which looked remarkably like the dreamstages in the dream-studio back in Slumberia. Right in front of her was some kind of giant rubber beanstalk. And next to that, suspended by ropes fifteen feet in the air, was a giant fiberglass foot.

Vivian liked this new world so much more than Slumberia. It was bright and warm, not dreary and dark. She liked the feverish bustle of this new world too. It was nothing at all like the lethargic thrum of Slumberia, where it always seemed as if everyone was just going through the motions. Best of all, Vivian had already seen and heard enough to know that this was a world that *appreciated* actors. Here Vivian Clavier could be a *real* star!

She paused to tread on an ant. That was another thing she liked about this new world: stepping on bugs. They didn't have those in Slumberia.

"Julie?" said a voice behind her. "Is that you?"

It was Julie's father. He was accompanied by a young girl—around Vivian's age, but really quite plain (though, unlike Julie, at least she had some decent clothes).

"Dad?" Vivian said, again talking in her sweetest Julie-voice.

"What are you *doing* here?" he asked, surprised.

"Half-day at school." Vivian tried her best to beam. "I figured I'd surprise you!"

"Well, honey, I wish you'd called me first."

Vivian nodded to the plain girl at his side. "Who's *this*, Dad?"

"Oh, I'm sorry," he said. "This is Lorna Leed. Remember the new television show I was telling you about? She's above-the-line."

"You mean one of the stars?" Vivian said.

He smiled happily. "Exactly."

"Hey," Lorna said to Vivian. She sounded as bored as she looked.

Vivian ignored her. Her mind was racing. Television show? She'd already learned enough to know that television was this world's version of dreams. And if there was a starring role for Lorna Leed, then that meant there was also a starring role for Vivian Clavier.

Providing, of course, that Lorna Leed doesn't get the part!

"Listen," her father was saying. "Let me just finish up with Lorna here, and then we'll get some lunch, okay? Why don't you wait in my office?"

"Okay!" Vivian chirped.

He and Lorna turned and walked along a path that led right underneath the giant hanging fiberglass foot.

Vivian glanced at the ropes that held the foot up in the air. They rose up to a pulley, and then angled down to an anchor right near Vivian.

She leaned over and unhooked the rope—then turned to watch the giant fiberglass foot plunge down right on top of poor Lorna Leed, who would never even know what hit her.

)

BACK IN Castle Alucard, Julie and her friends went for the big picture window. Roman threw the window open, and Meg sank down the outside castle wall on one of her silk lines.

Julie, Bentley, and Roman quickly followed after her. The silk felt soft to the touch, but was strong enough to hold them all.

Once they reached the ground far below, Meg somehow twisted the line so it dropped down after them. Up above, the Trull finally arrived in the parlor of the dream-producer. Their frustrated snarls echoed out through the open window. Julie still hadn't gotten a look at the creatures!

But for the time being, Julie and her friends were safe.

They were standing in a narrow canyon on the other side of the castle. The canyon walls were barely seven feet apart, but at least twenty feet tall. While crawling down Meg's silk line, Julie had seen that it was part of a whole network of twisting gullies that meandered outward, like cracks in dried mud, as far as the eye could see.

"It's like some kind of natural maze," Julie said.

Her words echoed, bouncing back and forth between the narrow canyon walls. *Maze . . . maze . . . maze . . .*

"But what if there's no way out?" said Roman. *No way out . . . no way out . . . no way out . . .* "We have to get you back to the dream-studio. And something tells me we haven't seen the last of the Trull."

Trull . . . Trull . . . Trull . . .

Julie thought for a second. "How much time do we have before moonset?"

Roman glanced up at the moon, which was still visible even over the lip of the canyon wall. "At least eight hours. Why?"

"The dream-producer said that it's the dream-executives in Nightmare City who really control the dreams." Julie had lowered her voice, but it echoed anyway.

"So?" said Roman.

"So I have to go to Nightmare City! I have to convince the dream-executives to stop making the nightmares!"

Nightmares . . . nightmares . . . nightmares . . .

"But Julie," said Roman, "what if something goes wrong? You heard what the dream-producer said. You'd be stuck here in Slumberia forever. And what about Vivian—how she's on the loose back in your world?"

Julie thought about this, but the answer was clear. If she couldn't somehow get the nightmares stopped, she didn't *want* to go back to her world. Vivian could have her old life, for all Julie cared. She had been on the verge of going crazy back there anyway.

"I have to do this," Julie said. "Somehow I *have* to stop the nightmares."

"But how do we get to Nightmare City?" asked Meg. "We don't even know the way out of this maze."

At that exact moment, something squeaked in the air over their heads. It was a knight-bird taking off from one of the dark towers of Castle Alucard, out into the pale moonlight. The dream-producer must have scheduled its departure before his untimely demise. It wasn't heading back to the dream-studio; it was heading in a new direction. But this made sense. The dream-producer had said that he communicated with the dream-executives in Nightmare City via knight-bird.

"That's *it*!" said Julie.

"What's it?" asked Bentley.

"The knight-bird," said Roman, cluing in. "If we follow it, it should lead us through the maze, all the way to Nightmare City."

"Exactly!" Julie said.

And with that, they turned and followed the bird as it flapped wearily into the night.

)

IT WASN'T hard to keep up with the metal bird. It was true that the winding canyons didn't always directly follow the path of the bird. But the creature moved at a slow pace. Even when Julie and her friends did happen to lose sight of it, they could always hear it squeaking in the dark. And the times that they went down blind alleys in the canyon labyrinth, the bird circled back at them, as if it were waiting for them to catch up.

They walked (and wiggled) in silence for a long time. It was cold and dark down in this maze of narrow canyons.

Finally, Meg said, "Can I make a confession?"

The words still echoed. *Confession . . . confession . . . confession.*

"Sure," Julie said.

"It's just that I'm *loving* this trip of ours!" The glowworm thought for a second. "Well, except for the almost-getting-eaten-by-a-vampire part."

Julie smiled. This wasn't what she had expected the worm to say. "Meg, what made you want to travel in the first place?"

"Oh, it was my mama, back where I grew up, on Moonshine Bay. She always used to talk about all the places she'd been, the things she'd done. She told us stories of how she'd gone exploring in the Midnight Jungle, and how she'd once climbed to the top of Mount Quintessence. She told us how she'd even gone all the way across the Brain Plain and the edge of the Neuronal Swamp.

"So why didn't you ever go?"

"Well, the Trull came to Moonshine Bay four years ago. They said that things had changed in Slumberia, that somebody called the dream-executives were in charge now, and they had this piece of paper that they wanted me to sign—some kind of contract. They said if I didn't sign it, they'd hurt my mama. So I signed their dumb ol' piece of paper. Then they gave me a choice: I could work in something called the dream-studio, as a spotlight. Or I could be the light at the top of a lighthouse. I figured that atop a lighthouse I could at least see the horizon, you know? I could watch it and dream of the places I could go. So that's what I chose. But there's just one thing about a horizon: you can't ever see over the darn thing. So it ended up just making things worse. A lot worse! It was a constant reminder to me of all the things I'd never done, and the places I could never go."

Never go . . . never go . . . never go. . . .

"That's terrible," Julie whispered. It wasn't only Meg's words that made Julie uneasy. There was something about the labyrinth itself. It was as if feelings echoed off the cold stone walls along with the sounds.

"Just who are these dream-executives anyway?" she asked the others. "Where did they come from?"

"From somewhere across the Sea of Emotion," Bentley said. "They came with the Trull about five years ago. The very first thing they did once they landed in Slumberia was come to us sharks saying they needed lawyers. Lots and lots of lawyers! They wanted us to sign contracts saying we'd help them. You'd think, as lawyers, we would have been smart enough to read the fine print, but we sharks are suckers for a little bloody chum. Anyway, once they had us sharks under contract, they had us write contracts for everyone else. That's when they took over the dream-studio and started building Nightmare City. I got assigned the moat at the dream-producer's castle. And ever since then, I've just been swimming in circles."

Swimming in circles . . . swimming in circles . . . swimming in circles . . .

Julie could feel Bentley's pain coming at her in waves.

"Still," Julie said, "I bet you're a great lawyer."

Bentley kicked the sand on the floor of the labyrinth.

"Nah. Oh, I've tried, I really have! But I never wanted to be a lawyer in the first place. I only went to law school because that's what my parents wanted me to do. As a lawyer, I'm a real jellyfish. I just don't have that 'killer' instinct. My dad still hasn't forgiven me for that sea cucumber investment fiasco. How was I to know there's no such thing as a sea pickle?"

"What did you want to do?" Julie asked.

"What?" Bentley said.

"You said you only went to law school for your parents. So what did you want to do?"

"Oh, you'll laugh."

Laugh . . . laugh . . . laugh . . .

"No, we won't," Julie said.

"Well," said the shark, "I wanted to help make Slumberia a better place. Either that or open a little bistro somewhere."

"Sometimes lawyers make things better."

"Please. Look at these teeth." Bentley bared his rows of yellow teeth, which glowed luminescent in the dark. "These weren't made for helping. They were made to rip and tear."

Rip and tear . . . rip and tear . . . rip and tear . . .

Julie could barely handle the sadness that washed over her now. The walls of the labyrinth didn't just cause emotions to echo; it also amplified them. Or maybe it was just that Julie was finally realizing how sad her friends really were.

"Roman?" Julie said.

"What?" he said.

"You're just being kind of quiet. What about you?"

"What about me?"

"Well, how did you end up working at the dream-studio?" His was the story she most wanted to hear.

But he stopped suddenly. "That's it," he said.

Julie was confused. She looked over at him in the dark. "What's it?"

He nodded forward.

The walls of the canyon had fallen away; the labyrinth had come to an end. In front of them, the black skyscrapers of Nightmare City rose so high into the hazy Slumberian sky that it looked like they almost touched the moon.

8

The Knight-Birds' Secret

THANK GOODNESS she's okay," Julie's father said, back at the television studio.

"Who?" Vivian asked.

"Lorna! What a relief that giant foot landed on her leg and not her head."

It was several hours after Lorna's "accident" with the hanging prop. Vivian and Julie's dad were having a late lunch in the studio commissary.

"I saw the rope slip," Vivian said. "I *tried* to stop it, but it was too late."

"Oh, honey, it wasn't your fault. There wasn't anything you could do." He picked at his chicken Caesar. "Of course, with her leg in a cast, it's violins and slow fade for Lorna."

So she's going to be fired, thought Vivian. It was exactly what she had intended.

"Ooooh!" Vivian cried. Aware that she might be overacting, she reined it in a bit. "That's too bad."

"This is a *disaster*," he said. "We were theme-song-ready, but now there's a blank line in our credit scroll. And we tape pilot in three days!"

Vivian understood every word that Julie's dad had said. He needed a replacement actress for Lorna. Fortunately, Vivian had the perfect actress in mind: herself!

The key was not to appear too eager. She took a delicate bite from her burger. Beef was much better than the only other thing she'd ever eaten in this world—Julie's mother's muffin, that morning. The beef was especially good rare.

Then, very quietly, Vivian said, "Hey, Dad, aren't I about the right age?"

"Hmm?" her dad said, still lost in his salad.

"I'm the same age as Lorna, right? Wouldn't that be something, my taking Lorna's place? It might even be fun, being here every day on the lot with you."

Her dad speared a crouton, obviously lost in thought.

Okay, thought Vivian. *It's time to bring out the big guns!*

"I suppose you're right," Vivian said casually. "I mean, Mom would go absolutely *nuts* if you let me audition. Can you imagine? We'd never hear the end of it."

Her dad looked up and stared at her. It was like Vivian could actually see the lightbulb going on over his head.

"You'd really want to audition for my television show?"

Vivian smiled, some to Julie's dad, but even more to herself.

)

NIGHTMARE CITY was all skyscrapers. There were dozens of them, narrow but impossibly tall, more like vertical stripes than buildings. The city may only have been a few years old, but it looked like something from a previous industrial age, all girders and black iron. The windows, meanwhile, were small, like square portholes or maybe arrow slits, and the only light behind them was a feeble yellow. One building in the middle towered even higher than the others.

The city had been built right at the edge of a dark sea. No wind blew off the water, and no waves rolled in from beyond the shore. The sea itself looked stagnant and even blacker than the city itself, more like thick crude oil than water.

Fluttering around the buildings of Nightmare City were hundreds upon hundreds of birds. Julie might have mistaken them for pigeons, except for the telltale squeak of their wings. They were knight-birds—some flying inland or back from there, and some flying off in other directions too, up and down the Slumberian coast or out across the ocean. But most were sluggishly flapping between buildings, or between different floors of the same building. Knight-birds weren't just being used to communicate with the dream-studio and the dream-producer. They were also being used to communicate around Nightmare City, and to other, distant locations too.

"All this just for my dreams?" Julie asked.

"I've heard they're branching out," Bentley said. "The dream-executives are in talks to increase production of something called 'daydreams.' And I've heard they've got plans to expand into 'delusions' and 'hallucinations.'"

As they entered the city, Julie saw that the streets were deserted. Discarded sheets of white paper littered the narrow streets, a sharp contrast to the coal-black skyscrapers. The papers were so thick that Julie couldn't see the pavement. The whole area smelled of rust and salt from a rancid sea.

"But where are the dream-executives?" Julie asked, taking it all in.

None of her friends answered. No one knew.

Julie glanced up at the moon, which was now five-eighths full. They'd been in that labyrinth of echoes for a full three hours!

Roman was looking at the moon too. "Five hours," he said. "That's how much time we have before moonset. And in that time, we have to find the dream-executives *and* get Julie all the way back to the dream-studio."

"That's not nearly enough time to check out all these buildings," said Bentley.

"We should ask directions!" suggested Meg.

"Of who?" Julie said. "The city's empty."

Suddenly a knight-bird crashed down into the white papers right in front of them. The paper, which was dry and brittle, crunched at the impact, with loose sheets flying every which way.

"I thought I recognized you folks!" said the bird.

"Greta!" Julie said. "What are you doing here?"

"Hey, it's on my route," said the bird. "But the real question is, what are *you* doing here?"

"We're here to see the dream-executives. Do you know where we can find them?"

Greta's body armor squeaked as she sat upright. "Now, why in the world would you want to see *them*? Never mind, I don't wanna know. But they're in Nightmare Central. That's the tallest building of 'em all, in the very middle of the city, and they're on the very top floor. I should know, I've flown up there enough times. Anyway, don't say I didn't warn you."

Julie couldn't resist asking the knight-bird one more question. "I'm sorry, but what *are* you exactly?"

"*Excuse* me?" said the bird.

"It's just that I don't know what's inside a knight-bird's armor. Are you a bird?"

"No, no, we ain't no stupid *birds*. We're grognits."

"Grognits?" Julie said.

The creature exaggerated a sigh that echoed inside the tin. "Oh, go ahead. Take a look. It's just that much longer before I have to go back to work."

"Really? I can look inside?"

"I said so, didn't I?"

Julie knelt down next to the knight-bird. There were slender gaps in the metal where the plates joined together. She peered through one of them.

The interior of the knight-bird was mostly hollow. But in

the very center was a miniature mechanical contraption, like the metal skeleton of a hang glider. It was attached to the body and wings of the knight-bird armor, so when it moved, the armor moved. And strapped tightly to the middle of that metal skeleton was a yellow butterfly.

"Oh!" said Julie, awestruck. "You're a butterfly!" No wonder the knight-birds were so tired! Inside each suit of armor was a single butterfly desperately trying to keep itself aloft.

"*Hey!*" said the creature. "I ain't no prissy butterfly neither!"

"Then what are you?"

"Already told you! A grognit."

"Well, what's the difference between a butterfly and a grognit?"

"Have you ever seen a butterfly with one of *these?*" Inside the knight-bird armor, Greta wiggled her upper lip.

"I don't—" Julie started to say.

"A mustache!" said Greta. "How many butterflies have you ever seen with a *mustache?*"

"Oh," said Julie. Greta *did* have a very tiny mustache on her upper lip. "It's true I've never seen a butterfly with a mustache." She hadn't seen many females with mustaches either, but decided it was best not to point this out.

"*That's* the difference between a butterfly and a grognit!"

"I'm curious," said Julie. "Did the dream-executives

make you sign a contract forcing you to work for them?" By now she had a pretty good idea how things were done in Slumberia.

"Sure did," said Greta. "And no time off for nectar breaks neither."

"My dad's always complaining that his workers are in something called a 'union,'" Julie said. "Have you thought about forming one of those?"

But suddenly Greta jerked upright with another squeak. She tilted her head to one side, as if listening.

"What is it?" Julie asked.

The knight-bird didn't answer, just started furiously flapping her wings. With a running start, she took off into the air, sheets of paper swirling in the air behind her.

"It's the Trull!" Greta called back. "Save yourselves! *Run!*"

Now Julie heard it too: the crumple of brittle paper under vicious claws. Then the roaring began. The Trull were right behind them, just around the corner.

Roman turned toward the center of the city. "This way!" he said.

But the crunch of sharp claws echoed from that direction too. Elephantlike roars trumpeted out both behind *and* in front of them.

The Trull had caught up with them again! And this time, they were surrounded. This time, there could be no escape.

9

The Truth About the Trull

VIVIAN STARED into Julie's closet, disgusted. She recognized all these clothes: Vivian had worn most of them as costumes in the various nightmares in which she'd starred. But she needed to make a good impression at tonight's audition for Julie's dad and the producers of his new television show, and there was nothing in that closet that didn't make her look like an eleven-year-old frump.

Vivian sensed she was being watched.

Julie's mother stood in the doorway of the bedroom.

"Why don't we color-wash your walls this weekend?" the woman said. "It'll give your bedroom a softer, gentler look, and the brushstrokes will add much-needed texture. I've got glaze and turpentine down in the basement."

"Really?" Vivian said brightly. "That would be *great*." What she really wanted to do with Julie's bedroom was lose the ridiculous wardrobe and ancient looking-glass, replacing them with something modern, and then maybe getting some decent blinds for the picture window. But that would have to come later.

Vivian turned back to the closet.

"What are you doing?" Julie's mother asked, stepping closer. Vivian regretted not shutting the door.

"Oh, I thought I'd go over to Lisa's tonight," Vivian lied casually. "We might go to the mall with her parents." She knew she couldn't tell Julie's mother the truth about the audition.

"When you get home, we can have some hot chocolate," said Julie's mother. "The key to a truly great cup of hot chocolate is real vanilla, orange zest, and a dash of salt."

Oh, this will simply not *do,* thought Vivian. For a career in television, she needed the father—for the time being anyway. But she didn't need hot chocolate and blueberry muffins every time she turned around. She didn't need the mother at all.

"Julie," said Julie's mother, next to her at the closet. "I want you to know that I'm aware how much your father and I have been arguing lately. I also want you to know that I know it's not fair to you, and I'm trying to be better."

Vivian decided right then that she had to take care of this woman—the same way she had taken care of Lorna Leeds.

She faced Julie's mother with a brave smile. "Oh, I *do* know how hard you try."

"Thank you, Julie," the mother said, choking up a little. "I also want you to know how much I love you."

"I love you too!" Vivian said, flinging her arms about the woman, even as she thought, *It won't do just to injure the mother, to get her temporarily sidelined, like Lorna Leeds.*

No, Vivian thought. *Julie's mother will have to be taken out for good!*

)

Fluffy white poodles.

That's what surrounded Julie and her friends on the streets of Nightmare City. There were four of them—two in front and two behind. They walked upright, standing about three feet tall. And they were dressed as security guards, with little blue uniforms and little police caps.

"I don't get it," Julie said to her friends, confused. "Where are the Trull?" She'd thought they were surrounded by them. She had heard their roars and the crunch of their claws against all the loose paper. Were they coming from somewhere behind these trained poodles?

"What do you *mean?*" Roman whispered. "They're right *there.*"

Roman's eyeballs looked like they were going to burst. He was staring at the fluffy white poodles like they were desert ghosts—or worse.

"Are you telling me," Julie said, "that *these* are the creatures that we've been running from all this time? With that scary roar?"

Roman could barely manage a nod.

Julie laughed out loud. "But they're not even wearing pants!"

"Julie," Roman said under his breath, "I don't think you understand—"

"Oh, I think I do!"

The poodles had edged closer now, forming a tight circle around Julie and her friends. The dogs stood there, their little kindling-like legs spread firmly apart. Julie faced them.

And then she saw their eyes.

They were as black as a deep cave on the dark side of the moon. As soft and gentle as Roman's eyes had looked when they'd first met, the eyes of these poodles were the exact opposite: hard and angry and mean.

And evil. Unquestionably evil.

A low growl rumbled in the throat of one of the dogs. It bared sharp yellow teeth.

"Oh!" Julie said. Suddenly she understood. The Trull's appearance was a lie. Any one of these creatures could leap up and rip all their throats wide open.

"What do you want?" Roman asked the Trull.

"Give us the girl!" yipped the lead dog, his face a wicked grimace. "If you do, we'll let the rest of you live!"

"That's crazy!" said Meg.

"Out of the question!" said Roman.

There was a pause while Meg and Roman looked over at

Bentley, who had opened his briefcase and was ruffling through some papers marked *Last Will and Testament*.

"Oh!" the shark said quickly. "Yes, of course, what they just said!"

Julie knew she had to do something. She couldn't have her friends sacrificing themselves for her!

And so she slouched. She placed her hands limply on her waist. She mustered up her snippiest voice and said to the dogs, "What *exactly* do you think you're doing? Do you have any idea who I *am*?"

Julie was pretending to be Vivian. It was their only hope. She had seen how Vivian had acted at her school—how she had taken control of the place through the sheer force of her will. If it had worked there, it could work here too. After all, she and Vivian looked exactly alike.

"Ms. Clavier?" said the lead poodle. "Is that you?"

"Of course it's me, you *idiot*!" Julie said. "Who did you *think* it was?"

With her hands on her hips and her nose in the air, she commanded the attention of Roman, Meg, Bentley, and all four of the Trull.

Julie had never felt so helpless in her entire life. Just because she and Vivian looked alike, that didn't mean they *were* alike, not by a long shot.

"We were told to find a mousy-looking girl and a dark-haired boy," the head Trull said. "We were told to eliminate her."

Eliminate? Julie thought. *Vivian really meant business!*

But outwardly, Julie just sighed loudly. "No, you idiots, you've been chasing *me*! First I went to visit the dream-producer at Castle Alucard, and now I've come here to Night-mare City to meet with the dream-executives."

The Trull glanced at each other, dark eyes darting back and forth. But they didn't attack. As they shuffled their little feet ever so slightly, the loose paper on the ground crinkled. The Trull were at least considering her story. But could they also smell fear, like most dogs? Julie hoped not, because she had to be reeking with fright right then.

"You *obviously* got your trail mixed up back at the dream-studio," Julie said. "Isn't it obvious? Besides, you're looking for two people—a girl and a boy—right? Well, there are *four* of us."

"It's true," the Trull said, "they didn't say anything about a shark and a glowworm, but—"

"'Glowworm'?" Julie said, eyes blazing. "Don't you know *anything*? This creature is obviously not a glowworm at all, but a silkworm! There's a big difference, you know. All glowworms are silkworms, but all silkworms are not glowworms!" Would they buy Julie's lies and evasions? Even she had to admit they were pretty lame. Of course, maybe it wasn't so much what she said as how she said it.

The Trull were twitchier than ever. "Well . . . ," said their leader. "If you're Vivian and not the girl and the boy, who are all these other people?"

She gestured to Roman. "This is my agent." She nodded at Bentley. "And my lawyer." Finally, she came to Meg. "And this silkworm happens to be my . . ." Julie wracked her brain. "The president of my fan club!"

Meg fluttered her eyelids and smiled adoringly.

"Now, I'm sorry," Julie said, straightening, "but I have an appointment with the dream-executives in Nightmare Central. So if you'll excuse me."

"I'm sorry, Ms. Clavier, but our orders are to make sure that—"

"Your *orders*?" Julie said. "Who do you think *gave* those orders? It was *me*, you idiot! And you screwed them up! But maybe if you go back to the dream-studio right now, you can still find the mousy-looking girl and the dark-haired boy!"

The Trull didn't budge. "Well, if we could just go check out your story with the dream-executives—"

"Are you *crazy*?" Julie shrieked. "Do you think the dream-executives have time to listen to a bunch of yapping teacups? I'm already late as it is. You guys are absolutely worthless. Forget I called you in the first place. I officially call off the flying monkeys! Now get your ratty, flea-infested hides back to the dream-studio."

The Trull still did not move.

Finally, one of the silent creatures spoke up. "Maybe she's right," it said. "Maybe we *did* follow the wrong trail. Maybe we should go back."

"Yes!" Julie said. "Maybe you *should*!"

Julie kept glaring at them until, one by one, they turned and headed sheepishly back the way they had come. They even had their little tails between their legs.

"That's better," she called after them, as sweetly as possible. "Maybe I'll even put in a good word about you to the dream-executives!"

)

THEY ENTERED Nightmare Central through a revolving door. The lobby inside was large, but dark and oppressive. The walls and ceiling were more black iron, buttressed by heavy girders, with some polished black stone lining the floor. The dim yellow light from the blocky fixtures could barely penetrate the darkness. It was dry and dusty, but not like the forgotten mustiness of Castle Alucard. This felt more like no one had ever been here to forget it in the first place. It felt completely lifeless.

But it wasn't entirely. A single Moon Person sat right inside, facing them from the receptionist's desk.

"Oh!" Julie said, surprised. "I thought the Moon People just worked at the dream-studio."

"No," said Bentley. "They also do the office work here in Nightmare City. The whole city's full of them."

"You mean all these skyscrapers are full of Moon People?" Julie said, appalled.

Bentley nooded. "Doing paperwork. Hey, there's a reason this place is called Nightmare City!"

Roman stepped up to the Moon Person receptionist. "We're here to see the dream-executives," he announced.

The face of the Moon Person was completely blank. It wasn't even a face. Like the Moon People Julie had seen before, the receptionist's giant head had no features. Up close, Julie saw vague bumps and pockmarks, but not where the eyes and mouth should have been.

It gave Julie the creeps. She didn't like not having any idea what was going on inside the Moon Person's head.

The creature merely pointed to the bank of heavy iron elevators.

"Thank you," Roman said politely.

)

THERE WAS an operator inside the elevator, of course.

A Moon Person operator.

He wore a blue uniform with brass buttons. From the neck down, he looked like a Christmas ornament, like the thinnest toy soldier ever built. But from the neck up, he had the same huge, featureless head as all the other Moon People.

Once they were all inside the elevator, Roman said, "Top floor, please." The Moon Person pulled a lever in the wall, and the doors rolled closed. But there were no numbered floor buttons. Instead, there were a couple of brass handles rising out of the floorboards. Without a word, the Moon Person began grinding on them, controlling the elevator like a carnival ride.

The elevator immediately shuddered and squeaked, then jerked into an upward motion. The gears of the elevator whirred just over their heads. Julie smelled lubricating oil and the sizzle of electricity.

No one said anything. On the other side of a little glass window in the door, floors flashed by, slowly at first, but then faster and faster, until they flickered almost as fast as a movie image.

This was the closest Julie had ever been to one of the Moon People. She was dying to get a better look at his featureless face. Still, she didn't want to be rude.

Out of the corner of her eye, she peeked over at his head.

The whole thing was coarse and cratered, exactly like the moon. But as she stared at it, Julie suddenly thought she saw vague facial features—a small lump of a nose, and maybe even the curve of a mouth. She turned to get a better look.

They *were* features! There were widely spaced eyes, a long mouth, even nostrils for the nose. How had she not noticed them before? And did *all* the Moon People have such features, or just this one?

Without warning, the elevator operator turned to her. Julie gasped in surprise. But she didn't look away. She *couldn't* look away, because she wasn't just seeing the features of the Moon Person; now she could make out his expression. And it was unlike anything Julie had ever seen.

The flat eyes looked sunken and hollow, the eyebrows drooped. The wide mouth was drawn and exhausted. It was the face of a person too sad and tired even to cry.

Suddenly the elevator lurched to a stop. They had apparently reached the top floor. The operator calmly turned and faced forward again, then he drew the switch, and the doors rumbled open.

Julie kept staring at the face of the elevator operator. But as suddenly as the elevator had stopped, the face on the Moon Person had disappeared. Once again, the face looked blank, like the surface of the moon.

"Julie?" said Roman. He and the others had already stepped out of the elevator.

"What?" said Julie, transfixed by the Moon Person's suddenly changing face. "Oh, right."

She followed the others out of the elevator. As the doors closed, the features on the face of the Moon Person remained invisible.

But the memory lingered, unsettling Julie. The face had looked so *sad*! And why had it suddenly appeared and disappeared like that? Was it something about the face of the Moon Person himself? Or was her ability to finally see the expression, if only for a moment, the result of something about Julie, something that had changed in her?

Julie had thought she'd wanted to know what was going

on inside the Moon People's heads, but now she wasn't so sure. The memory of that face made her feel cold inside, like the touch of the desert ghosts.

The top floor of Nightmare Central was bustling with people.

Many more Moon People.

Dozens of them trundled back and forth down the hallway. Glass walls revealed dimly lit offices full of more Moon People, most sitting, knees visible, in cramped metal cubicles typing at antique typewriters. Knight-birds hopped between the cubicles too, delivering messages and crawling in and out of small openings in the outside walls.

Roman pointed down the hallway. "There," he said. "That must be where the dream-executives meet."

A set of dark metal doors loomed up fifteen feet tall. Unlike the other offices, this one was windowless. It looked more like the entry to a dungeon than one to a conference room.

Julie looked at the Moon People shuffling around her. But to her surprise, suddenly she saw expressions on *all* their faces.

They each looked so impossibly sad! Julie had never seen such knitted brows, such grimly clenched jaws. And if their eyes had once been pools of emotion, they had long since dried up and were now dark and empty. Julie knew immediately why these faces looked the way they did: they were the expressions of beings with no hope.

This time, the features did not wink away again, like they had on the elevator operator. This time, Julie was confronted with faces of doom on all sides. But her friends weren't reacting to the scene, which meant that either they couldn't see the faces, or they'd been able to see them all along. Either way, Julie decided that, yes, something had changed in her that allowed her to see the faces clearly at last. Maybe, she thought, her journey through that labyrinth of echoes had made her more attuned to the feelings of those around her.

"Julie?" said Roman, nodding to the door at the end of the hall. "Shall we?"

"Right," she said, glad for a chance to be distracted from the faces of the Moon People.

They walked (and wiggled) to the giant double doors. An engraved brass sign hung from the door handles. It read, MEETING IN PROGRESS.

"I should go in alone," Julie said to her friends. "Why don't you all wait here?"

"Oh, that's crazy talk!" said Meg. "What's the point of coming all this way, but not seeing it through to the end?"

"And I *need* to go with you," said Bentley. He held up his briefcase. "You might need a lawyer!"

"And I'm definitely coming with you," said Roman. His brown eyes were as soft as always, but clearer than ever. He leaned forward and kissed Julie on the cheek. "Good luck. I hope you find what you're looking for."

She blushed, flustered. She'd just been kissed by a boy for the very first time!

Not knowing what else to do, she reached down and pulled open one of the doors, revealing the utterly bizarre sight of the conference room beyond.

The Bottom Line

THE SOUNDSTAGE was as silent as a tomb. Vivian had just finished her screen test for the role on Julie's dad's new television show. She was standing in front of a bare backdrop facing not just the cameras, but also the hip young men and women—the studio executives—who had come to watch her audition.

Vivian had completely nailed it. She knew it, and the executives knew it. She'd been certain she had the part even before the stunned silence. She felt it in her bones.

Sure, it wasn't the best part in the world, but at least it would get her on this thing called television. And that would lead to more parts. *Better* parts. Parts that would make her the star she was truly meant to be.

One of the executives spoke at last—to Julie's dad. "Where in the world did she learn to act like that?"

"I have no idea," said Julie's father. He looked out at her. "Julie? Where *did* you learn to do that?"

But Vivian just smiled demurely, exactly as she had practiced so many times. "Does that mean I wasn't completely horrible?"

"Horrible?" another one of the executives said. "You were absolutely sensational!"

"No!" Vivian said, pretending to be shocked. "Really?" But what she was thinking was, *If you think that performance was good, just wait until you see me when we get around to negotiating my contract!*

)

THE CONFERENCE room of the dream-executives looked like a television showroom. Rather than walls, it had banks of silent, flickering television screens, all exactly the same size. The room itself was one long rectangle, about sixty feet by twenty feet, and TV monitors covered every inch of wall space, and even the ceiling. Each of the televisions was tuned to a different channel—thousands of channels in all.

The only light in the room came from the television screens. The tidal wave of frenetic images overwhelmed Julie.

But amid the silent kaleidoscope of colors, she heard voices.

"Well, it certainly *is* cause for concern," said the first voice. "These latest figures show she sleeps forty minutes less than she did a year ago—and forty percent less than she did nine years ago." It was the voice of a young man.

"She was two years old nine years ago," said a second voice, another young man. "Of *course* she slept more then. We're not to blame for that. That's not a dream-production issue."

"I'm not so sure, Xavier," said the first voice. "I think part of the reason she's sleeping less is that she doesn't like the dreams."

Three figures sat huddled around a small conference table in the center of the room. Julie hadn't noticed them at first because they were all dressed in body-hugging black. They all sat looking the other way, so their faces were not visible. And they each wore some kind of shiny black helmet.

"So she may not like the dreams," said a third voice, a young woman, "but the bottom line is that she's watching—and she's remembering. That's the key. We're getting through to her waking mind. Remember when we used to give her happy dreams? She woke up and completely forgot why she felt so good. No, I say we keep doing exactly what we're doing."

"What if she stops sleeping entirely?" said the first voice. "Then where are we, Constance?"

Julie could barely believe her eyes—or her ears. Were these really the dream-executives? And were they really talking about *her* dreams?

One of the monitors on the wall snagged Julie's attention. It was a scene of her parents playing badminton with extra-large racquets. Julie was the birdie.

It was horrible, of course, seeing herself batted back and forth like that. But the scene looked . . . familiar.

It was one of Julie's dreams—from several weeks ago. It was all coming back to her now.

Another of the screens in the wall caught her eye. This time, Julie was baked into a birthday cake, and her parents were sharpening the knives they would use to slice her up.

Another one of her many recent nightmares.

Finally, Julie spotted a monitor displaying the dream from the night before. There she was on the giant chessboard, surrounded by living chess pieces.

That's when Julie knew: these *were* the dream-executives! And the scenes flickering on the television screens were all of her past nightmares.

"I think you're far too negative," the second executive—Xavier—was saying. "The feud between Julie's parents was the best thing that's ever happened to us. With a few changes, we can keep replaying this dream until the day she dies."

"That's not what the numbers show," said the first executive. "The numbers show we're losing our audience. And no matter what anyone says, we won't win her back through remakes and sequels."

"But it *is* working!" said Xavier. "We're getting through to her waking mind. That's all that matters. Why rock the boat? Stay with what works, that's what I always say."

"Right *now* it's working," said Constance—the female

executive. "But Damon is right, the overall trend is very bad. We need to be bold, we need to shock. Times like these are the very worst times to play it safe."

"So what are you saying?" Xavier asked.

"I'm saying we need to move it up a notch," Constance said. "Push the envelope a little. Maybe even a lot."

"Excuse me," Julie said quietly.

"Push the envelope *how*?" said Xavier, completely ignoring Julie.

"How else?" said Constance. "More violence. Frankly, I think we've been way too cautious. Why exactly are we holding back?"

"Constance is absolutely right," Damon said. "That's the problem with violence: a person gets used to it. Over time, the violence loses its impact. But the obvious solution to that problem is to make the violence *more* graphic, *more* horrible. After all, when it comes to violence in nightmares, the sky's pretty much the limit, right?"

More *violence in my nightmares?* Julie thought. Could that really be what the dream-executives were saying?

"*No!*" she shouted.

All three figures pivoted around to look at her. Julie gasped when she finally saw their faces.

They weren't wearing shiny black helmets; those helmets were their actual *heads*—like bowling balls balanced on their necks. And in the very center of each of those black shiny balls, exactly where the face should have been, was yet another television monitor. The video image of a face flickered out from each screen—or rather, a video image of bits and pieces of dozens of different faces. A young man's lips. An old man's nose. A baby's chin. But each piece of face quickly faded away, to be replaced by a piece from yet another face. It was unnerving, because even though the general shape of the faces remained more or less constant, the individual pieces—the cheeks and lips and eyebrows and earlobes—were constantly changing.

"What do *you* want?" said Damon, sitting on the right. "Can't you see we're very busy?" The voice emerged from a little speaker underneath the television monitor. Meanwhile, the parts of the face on the screen quickly changed—lips became pursed, eyes narrowed—into features of annoyance.

"You can't do it!" Julie said. "You can't make the nightmares even worse! Don't you see? It's not *right!*"

There was a moment's pause, then Xavier, sitting in the middle, said, "Where were we?" And all three dream-executives simply spun their chairs back around to face the conference table.

"Let's brainstorm," Damon said. "What about starting production on a nightmare where Julie gets drawn and quartered by her parents? We can give it an Old West theme, with her mom on one horse and her dad on another."

"Or something about her parents as stage magicians?"

Constance said. "They can argue over who gets to cut her in half, and then, of course, things go horribly wrong."

"Not bad," Xavier said thoughtfully. "But I think we're still holding back."

"*Please!*" Julie said. "I couldn't handle those dreams! I can barely handle them as they are!"

"Would someone please get this girl out of here?" called Constance in a singsong voice, to no one in particular.

"We don't care what *you* think!" Damon said, with not even a glance toward Julie. "Believe me, we *know* our audience!"

At this, Julie lost it.

"But don't you *see*? I *am* your audience! *I'm* Julie Fray— the girl you've been talking about for the last five minutes! It's me! Here! In Slumberia! Right in front of you! And I've come to ask you to *please* stop making nightmares!"

The dream-executives turned around to peer at her again. The flickering screens on the walls around Julie reminded her of a thousand eyeballs all staring right at her. But this time, to Julie's surprise, the features on the faces of the dream-executives seemed to be rearranging themselves into expressions of interest.

"I like it," said Constance. "The girl's got spunk."

"She looks like her too," said Damon, adding in a perfectly loud voice, "I assume we can do something about the hair?"

"I think it's high time we stop kidding ourselves about Vivian," said Xavier. "Lately, she's just phoning it in."

"Vivian's not going to take this lying down," said Damon. "And she has an ironclad contract. She's one *heck* of a negotiator."

"Don't worry about Vivian," said Constance. "We can handle her."

Xavier looked back at Julie. "Did you bring a résumé?" he asked.

Julie shook her head. "No, you don't understand. I don't want the *part* of Julie. I *am* Julie! I've crossed the wall between the waking and sleeping minds!"

Again, the dream-executives stared at her, their faces still flickering, but not with interest anymore. They were already bored with her.

"Security!" Damon called. "Please get this girl out of here!"

"No, wait!" Julie said.

But it was too late. The doors to the conference room slammed open, and four new Trull burst inside, ready to haul Julie and her friends away.

Mourning in Slumberia

JULIE WAS sitting on an upside-down bucket. She and her friends had been locked inside a storage room on the top floor of the highest building in Nightmare City. "Take them away!" the dream-executives had said to the Trull. "We'll deal with them later. Put them somewhere where they can't escape." The Trull had done just that, shoving Julie and her friends into this dark little room full of mops and a floor-waxing machine and shelves lined with extra rolls of paper towels.

Roman slammed his shoulder against the door of the room. For well over an hour, he had been trying to force his way out. But he turned to Julie, exhausted. "It's no use. I can't get it open."

Julie nodded glumly. "It's okay."

"Well, I'm already planning one heck of a lawsuit against the dream-executives!" Bentley said. "The way the Trull treated us? I've got a case of whiplash that you wouldn't *believe*."

"But even if we did sue them . . ." Julie didn't finish her thought. She glanced up at a tiny window in the back of the storeroom.

The moon was over seven-eighths full. They'd never make it back to the dream-studio before moonset now, no matter how hard they ran (and wiggled). There just wasn't enough time. Which meant that Julie was stuck in Slumberia forever.

"Julie," said Roman. "I'm so sorry."

She tried to smile. "Oh, it's okay. If I have to stay here in Slumberia, at least I'll be here with my friends. At least we'll be together."

Julie's friends all looked away at exactly the same time.

"What?" Julie asked.

Roman shook his head. "Nothing. It's nothing."

"Tell me. Are you saying we won't be together? That we all can't get jobs at the dream-studio, or here at Nightmare City?"

"That might happen," Roman said quickly. Too quickly.

"Absolutely!" Meg said.

"Sure!" Bentley said. "Makes perfect sense!"

But Julie knew her friends weren't telling the truth. "You're all going to be punished, aren't you?"

"No!" Roman said—again, too quickly. "Of course not!"

"That's crazy talk!" Meg said.

"Ridiculous!" Bentley said.

"Come on, you guys," said Julie. "Tell me the truth."

There was a moment's pause as her three friends eyed each other. Then Roman mumbled, "I suppose I might be written up by a supervisor."

The glowworm shrugged. "Maybe I'll get a few demerits here and there."

And Bentley casually waved his webbed fingers. "Some little note might be put in my file somewhere."

Julie stared at them all. Once again, no one was looking her in the eye.

"The truth!" she demanded. She would settle for nothing less.

Roman sighed, long and low; and yet in some strange way, he sounded relieved. "By coming with you," he said, "we violated our contracts."

"You?" Julie said to Roman, surprised. "You're under a contract too?"

He nodded once.

Of course *Roman is under contract!* thought Julie. Everyone else was. It only made sense that he would be too.

"The Trull came for me when I was just a boy," he explained, eyes on the floor. "They said they wanted me to work in the dream-studio. My parents said no. They tried to fight, but the Trull took them away. I tried to fight too, but I was too small. There was nothing I could do. I was powerless. I never saw my parents again."

Julie's heart exploded like a dandelion in the wind. "Oh, Roman!" she said. "I'm so sorry."

"It's okay, Julie. It was a long time ago. Anyway, since the three of us have broken our contracts, we'll be punished."

"Punished *how*?" Julie asked.

"They'll send us to this island," Bentley said.

"An island?" Julie said. "What kind of island?"

"Well, I suppose some might call it a kind of a prison."

"A prison!"

"Oh, now, it ain't that bad," Meg said. "That lighthouse was just another kind of prison anyway."

"And so was the moat," said Bentley.

"And so was the dream-studio," added Roman.

Julie could hardly believe her ears. Her friends were being sent to prison because of her. "I wish I'd never asked you guys to come with me!"

"You didn't ask," Roman said. "I decided. And if I had to do it again, I'd do the same thing all over."

"Me too!" said Meg.

"And me," said Bentley.

"But why?" Julie asked.

"Well, I wanted to travel," said the glowworm. "And so I did."

"I wanted out of that darn moat," said the shark. "And now I am."

"And I was tired of being powerless," said Roman. Tears dripped from his eyes. If the eyes of the Moon People had been bone-dry of all feeling, Roman's were not. They were two swirling wells of emotion, spilling over at last. "Julie, don't you see? By helping you all these years after they took my parents, it was like I was finally able to fight back."

"But it was all for nothing," Julie whispered. "You'll all be punished."

Roman dried his eyes. "It wasn't for nothing. For one day at least, the three of us knew again what it was like to be free."

Julie turned away. It was all she could do to keep from crying.

"I wonder what Vivian's been up to back in my world," Julie said, changing the subject.

"Oh!" Roman said suddenly. "I almost forgot." He reached into the pocket of his jumpsuit and pulled out a shard of broken glass.

Not glass. *Mirror.* The reflected moonlight glinted in her eyes.

"It's a piece of the Mirror of the Minds," Roman explained. "I picked it up back at the dream-producer's castle. I thought maybe it would come in handy."

"Do you think it still works?" said Meg.

"I'm not sure," said Roman, even as Julie and the others gathered around.

For a moment, nothing happened. But then an image formed on the surface of the glass.

It was the kitchen at Julie's house. Vivian and Julie's father had just come in from the garage.

"Honey, I'm just *so* proud of you!" Julie's dad was saying.

"You were Golden Globe good tonight. I don't think I've ever been so happy you're my daughter."

Julie felt a sharp pang of jealousy. Her dad was proud of *Vivian*? She couldn't remember him ever saying he was proud of anything Julie had done, except to annoy her mom.

"I still can't believe you're going to be the star of my new television show!" he went on.

Her father had hired Vivian for his show? Somehow this made perfect sense. It also made Julie dizzy. She needed to sit back down on that upside-down bucket. Meanwhile, in the mirror, her father tenderly took Vivian's hand.

"And honey?" he said. "From now on, I'm going to try to get along better with your mother. I promise. I know it's long overdue."

"Oh, Dad!" exclaimed Vivian, throwing her arms around him in a tight embrace. "That makes me so happy!"

Suddenly Julie thought she might need the bucket she was sitting on to throw up in. How could her dad not see that that wasn't his daughter? Vivian was acting *nothing* like her! But maybe that was why her dad liked her so much, Julie thought bitterly.

"I'll be upstairs in a minute, okay?" said Vivian in the mirror. "I think I want a snack."

"Okay," Julie's dad said, turning to go.

This was Julie's worst nightmare: seeing that her parents liked Vivian better. What could be worse than that?

"What is she doing now?" asked Meg, peering into the mirror.

Julie's father was gone. Vivian, meanwhile, took a tin of turpentine and a plastic funnel from under the sink. She grabbed a container of chocolate sauce from the refrigerator and began pouring the turpentine inside.

"Wait," Julie said. "That's what my mom uses to make her hot chocolate. But isn't turpentine poison? Why would Vivian—"

"Julie?" In the mirror, Julie's mother called down from upstairs. "Are you ready for our hot chocolate?"

Vivian placed the poisoned chocolate sauce back into the refrigerator, then hid the turpentine. "Ready!" she said sweetly.

Julie's eyes went wide with horror. "Vivian's trying to poison my mother!"

"What?" Roman said.

"She must have decided that she didn't need my mom, just my dad!" Julie whirled for the door. "We have to get out of here! I have to get home before Vivian poisons my mom!"

"Listen," Roman said suddenly. "I hear something."

Julie listened too. A key was being slid into the lock on the storeroom door. The knob jiggled, and the door opened.

A man in a janitor's uniform stared in at them from the other side of the doorway. He had a janitor's cart next to him.

"Just as I suspected," he said. "I thought this room might be occupied."

Julie did a double-take. It was the dreamwriter!

"What are *you* doing here?" she asked.

The dreamwriter sighed and held up a broom. "What does it look like?"

"You clean office buildings too?"

"Tuesdays and Thursdays. What can I say? The dream-executives don't much like writers."

"But how did you know we'd be here?"

"I told you before. I'm a writer, so I always know what's happened, and what's going to happen next." He reached for a dustpan from the wall of the storage room. "I'm also letting you go. So go on. Get out of here."

"You mean . . . ?"

"Why not?" said the dreamwriter.

"But the dream-executives!" she objected.

"Hey," he said, "I'm the writer here. If the dream-executives want a different plot twist, let 'em write it themselves!"

)

IN THE office hallway outside the storeroom, Roman turned to Julie. "Now what? We still don't have enough time to get you back to the dream-studio before moonset."

"Oh, yes, we do!" said Julie excitedly. "We have at least

thirty minutes until moonset. And knowing my mother, it'll take at least that long for her to make her homemade hot chocolate. But I have a plan to get me back by then—and put a few other things right too! Let's go!"

She hurried down the hallway with Roman, Meg, and Bentley right behind. She stopped and entered the first of the glass-walled offices.

"Hello!" she called out. "My name is Julie Fray, and I've come to stop the dream-executives. But I'll need your help!"

Dozens of Moon People sitting in dozens of cramped gray cubicles ceased their activity. They all looked up at her. The knight-birds also stopped what they were doing to listen.

The expressions on the faces of the Moon People were all just as clear as before, and just as sad. But as Julie continued to speak, she saw, on a couple of those faces, what seemed to be the faintest flickers of hope.

Morning in Slumberia

INSIDE THE conference room of the dream-executives, the thousands of television screens still glowed like giant radioactive eyeballs. The three executives still sat talking at their conference table.

"Okay, picture this," said Xavier, using his hands to frame an imaginary scene. "Julie's parents are both grinding hamburgers for two different barbecues—"

Julie and her friends strode into the room.

"Excuse me," Julie interrupted.

None of the dream-executives took any notice of her.

"I see where you're going with this!" Constance said to Xavier breathlessly. "And Julie gets too close to the grinders and she—"

"Excuse me!" Julie said, louder.

The three executives stiffened in their seats. As one, they swung around in their swivel chairs.

"You again!" snarled Constance.

"I'm here to make some demands," Julie said. "I want you to free the Moon People, the glowworms, the grognits, and anyone else you've managed to make into slaves. It isn't fair that they do all the work while you sit here in your office talking."

For a moment, the room was silent. Then facial features of glee erupted onto the monitors of the dream-executives. A second later, laughter exploded from their little speakers.

"I *mean* it!" Julie said over the laughter. "You're going to rewrite the contracts!"

"Or *what*?" asked Damon. "What could *you* possibly do?"

"Someone call Security," said Xavier.

"Never mind," said Constance. "Here they come now."

Two Trull strolled in through the open doors behind Julie.

She smiled. "This is your last chance," she said. "Promise me you'll rewrite the contracts—or else."

More laughter burst from the speakers of the dream-executives. "Or else *what*?" blubbered Constance.

The Trull took a step closer.

"Now!" Julie shouted.

Suddenly every television screen on the walls of the room flared up at the same time, then went stone-dead. The room fell into complete darkness. The laughter of the dream-executives stopped just as suddenly. For a confused moment, they sat there like mushrooms, too stunned to say or do anything at all.

"What's the meaning of this?" said Damon, from out of the blackness.

"*Security!*" shouted Constance.

Somewhere in the dark, a poodle whimpered.

A gentle breeze blew across the conference room.

"Something's wrong," said Damon. "I feel a draft."

"That's *impossible,*" said Constance. But even as she said this, a powerful gust swept through the room.

"This can't be!" said Xavier. "The grognits are all under contract with us. There *can't* be a breeze!"

The floor creaked.

"Who's there?" said Damon uneasily. "Wait, there's someone next to me! Who *are* you? Who gave you permission to be in here?"

Julie smiled at the dream-executives' confusion.

"Something very *odd* is going on here," said Xavier.

Without warning, a furious wind washed into the room. Clouds of small flapping creatures burst through the open doorway, and from vents up near the ceiling.

"Ouch!" cried Constance as wings fluttered all around. "Something just grabbed me!"

"Aarrg!" howled Xavier. "Something's *holding* me!"

"Un*hand* me!" demanded Damon.

Then, as quickly as it had come, the cloud of winged creatures settled lightly to the ground.

"Meg," Julie said softly. "Light, please."

The worm began to glow, quickly growing bright enough to light the room. Each of the dream-executives was being restrained by Moon People—three per executive. The expressions on the faces of the Moon People were as determined as they were hopeful.

Meanwhile, every surface of the conference room was now covered by colorful, butterflylike grognits, free from their knight-bird armor. (And as far as Julie could tell, they all had tiny mustaches on their upper lips!) They gently flexed their wings, as if in warning.

"The grognits!" hissed Xavier.

"And the Moon People!" said Constance. "What's the meaning of this?"

"I had a little talk with the staff right before coming in here," Julie said. "The grognits spread the word, and everyone agreed with me that your contracts aren't fair. So we want to change them."

"Ridiculous!" thundered Damon.

"Out of the question!" snapped Constance.

"Well," said Julie with a sigh. "Then I'm afraid the Moon People and the grognits are officially on strike."

"You'll never get away with this!" said Xavier. "The Trull will get you!"

Julie turned to the two Trull standing by in the conference room. They too were being restrained by the Moon People—six per security guard—and were also covered by gently flapping grognits. The Trull struggled and whimpered in vain.

Julie shook her head. "No, I don't think we'll have much of a problem with the Trull."

"I don't understand!" said Constance. "What do you want from *us*?"

Julie sauntered calmly to the conference table—with Roman, Bentley, and Meg right behind. "Bentley?" she said. "Get out your pad. I need you to write something up."

Bentley straightened. "You mean . . . ?"

Julie grinned. "I told you a lawyer could help make the world a better place."

Bentley swallowed, and then stepped up to the conference table. He snapped open his briefcase and withdrew a pad of yellow paper and a pen. "Ready."

Julie addressed the dream-executives. "What I want," she said with the sweetest of smiles, "is to rewrite a few contracts."

)

TEN MINUTES later, the three dream-executives signed the new contract, written by Bentley, releasing the citizens of Slumberia from their enslavement and revoking the executives' decision-making authority. After signing, the three dream-executives sat slumped at their conference table, utterly helpless. Bits and pieces of faces, alternately angry and despairing, faded in and out on their facial monitors.

"But if these three don't control the dream-production anymore," Bentley said, "who *does*? We may not need any more dream-executives, but we at least need another dream-producer."

"Write down Roman's name in the new contract," Julie said.

"What?" Roman said. "Don't be ridiculous! I don't have any experience for a thing like that."

Julie laughed. "Of course you do! Don't you remember what the dream-producer said? That a producer makes wishes come true? He may have been a vampire, but he was right about that."

"But I—"

"I told you my wish—that I wanted to stop my nightmares—and you made it come true. You brought me to the dream-producer, then all the way to Nightmare City, until I finally did stop the nightmares. You had courage and determination, you never lost your cool, just like a good dream-producer. Of course, before you get too busy producing my dreams, you'll have to take some time off to go look for your parents."

Julie watched while Bentley scratched the boy's name into the contract. But even as the room throbbed in the light of Meg's glow, Roman's face darkened.

"What's wrong?" Julie asked.

"I'm not such a great producer after all," he said miserably. "I didn't get you back to the dream-studio in time to save your mother."

"Don't worry about that. We'll make it."

"But how? There isn't enough time."

Julie's eyes sparkled. "There is if we *fly*! Greta, any chance you can give us a lift?"

"Sure!" Greta said, fluttering nearby.

Dozens of grognits immediately landed on Julie's shoulders and back. They latched their tiny hands onto her clothing and began flapping.

Slowly, they lifted Julie into the air. She had correctly predicted that if the grognits could carry all that knight-bird armor, they could surely lift her too!

Other grognits grabbed hold of Roman, Meg, and Bentley. Then they flapped furiously, carrying Julie and her friends directly to the nearest window, which they somehow squeezed through.

"Second star to the right and straight on till morning!" Julie said excitedly.

"What are you going on about?" said Greta. "That's not the way back to the dream-studio!"

"Sorry," said Julie. "I'll let you drive."

☽

SOMETHING WAS wrong with the Slumberian air. Or, rather, something was finally *right* with it. As the tiny grognits flew

Julie and her friends away from the skyscrapers of Nightmare City, the night air, which had once been so still and stale, swirled with fresh breezes and warm currents.

"That feels *wonderful!*" said Julie. "What happened?"

"Grognit wings!" said Greta. All around, colorful grognits flitted about in the open air.

"You mean . . . ?"

"Yup! The wind comes from grognit wings. But we couldn't get anything going trapped inside the knight-bird cages."

Behind them, something groaned.

"Look," Roman said, hovering nearby, pointing back at Nightmare City.

The city was sinking. The streets were already underwater, and all the black skyscrapers were quickly following them down. This was the sound they'd heard: the iron buildings were creaking and whining as they sank into the ocean.

"What's happening?" Julie said.

"Just what I was afraid of," Bentley said. "Nightmare City only existed on paper. By setting the Moon People and grognits free, we upset its perfect balance. Now the whole city's going under."

"Did the Moon People all get away?" Julie asked.

"With the grognits' help!" said Greta, nodding to the huge crowd of Moon People who had gathered on the beach beyond the sinking city. Seeing Julie, the crowd broke into a chorus of spontaneous cheering and waving. Julie knew they weren't actually making any noise, but somehow she knew exactly how they would sound.

"And the dreamwriter?" Julie asked.

"Over here!" said a voice. The dreamwriter was nearby, also being carried away by grognit wing.

"*Now* what?" Roman said, looking back at Nightmare City.

The bottom third of the city had disappeared underwater. But as the buildings sank, three black figures leapt from the roof of the tallest building. Almost immediately, gold-colored parachutes opened above each of them, and they began gliding away.

"It's the dream-executives!" Meg said.

As Nightmare City disappeared into the ocean, the wind blew the three dream-executives in their golden parachutes out to sea, which now roiled with waves and currents.

"Oh, no!" Julie said. "They're being blown out over the water!"

"There are plenty of sharks in the Sea of Emotion," Bentley said, "and lots of other nasty creatures too." He thought for a second and then added, "From everything I've seen of the dream-executives, I think they'll fit in just fine."

)

As JULIE and her friends soared over the hills beyond the coastline, a pale pink light peeked up over the eastern horizon. The gently twinkling Slumberian stars, which had only appeared when the grognit wind finally blew away the overhead haze, were already beginning to fade in the morning sunrise.

Sunrise? Julie thought. *Morning?* It was supposed to be *moonset!* Slumberia didn't even *have* a sun—or at least so Roman had implied.

He noticed the rosy light too. "Wait," he said thoughtfully. "That looks familiar."

"It's the Slumberian sun!" Bentley said.

"Oh, yes. I remember now from when I was a boy. But where did it come from?"

"The new contracts," the shark said smugly. "The dream-executives thought that daylight would be distracting, so they wrote it out of the old ones. It was one of the first things I changed."

"But something still isn't right," Julie said. "I thought it was supposed to be 'moonset.' I thought we had to get back to the dream-studio before Vivian went to bed. How can it be morning in Slumberia if it's nighttime in my world?"

"I think it must be reversed," Bentley said. "When it's nighttime in our world, it's daytime in yours. And when it's daytime in our world, it's nighttime in yours."

"Oh," said Julie, but something else occurred to her. "Then that means Vivian has already gone to bed! That means the breach in the wall between my waking and sleeping minds has already healed!"

"Not yet," said Roman. He pointed. A pale crescent moon was still visible despite the rising sun.

"Hurry, Greta!" said Julie.

"Don't you worry!" huffed Greta. "I'll get you back in time!"

)

As THEY sailed over the Slumberian landscape, Meg nodded down to the ground. "Look!"

Flowers were unfolding from the dirt at an incredible speed. There were crocuses and tulips and daffodils and bluebells and irises, and, unfortunately, a few dandelions.

Off to the left, a vast lake shimmered in the morning sunlight. Julie didn't recognize the body of water until she saw Meg's white lighthouse.

"The Lake of Creativity!" she said. "It's full again!"

"Another thing I changed in the contract," Bentley said proudly. "The dream-executives had taken most of the creative juices for themselves, diverting the flow from the brain."

The sights and sounds were all extraordinarily beautiful, but Julie was relieved when the dream-studio finally came into view. She could see the creative juices tower rising up above it all.

At Julie's direction, the grognits gently set Julie and her friends down right on top of the tank. There was just enough room for all of them to stand upright, but the top sloped precariously.

"Careful," Roman said to the gathering.

Julie searched the air for the breach in the wall between her waking and sleeping minds.

"I can't *find* it," Julie said, beginning to panic.

She glanced over at the sky. The moon had disappeared at last.

"Oh, no!" she exclaimed. "Moonset!"

They were too late. The rip had healed. Now Julie was stuck in Slumberia for good—and her mother was going to drink the poisoned hot chocolate and die!

13

A Nightmare Come True

No," Roman said, standing on the top of the creative juices tower. "We can't give up. Not yet."

Julie and her friends kept desperately scanning the air above the tank for any sign of the breach.

"I still don't see it!" Julie moaned.

But then Roman pointed. "There."

Julie didn't see anything. She kept squinting.

There *was* something there! It was vague, almost transparent now, but the spot was real.

She reached up on tiptoes to feel it. It was pliable, but soft, like a half-inflated inner tube. The surface was smooth like a scar.

Julie poked at it, but it seemed solid. There was no more actual hole.

"It's healed over!" Julie said.

"Well, don't just stand there!" Meg said. "Tear it open again!"

"With what? I need something sharp."

"There must be something down in the dream-studio," said Roman, scrambling for the ladder.

"There's no time!" said Meg. She looked up at Bentley. "Use those jaws of yours for something other than talk, and start gnawing!"

"Huh?" said Bentley.

"Your teeth! You're a shark, ain't you?"

"Oh, right!"

He opened wide, flashing row upon row of razor-sharp teeth.

Julie and Roman boosted him up.

"Now go to it!" Meg ordered.

Bentley snapped his jaws down hard on the breach and began gnawing.

"Harder!" said Meg. "Let 'er rip!"

Suddenly the black spot reappeared. It throbbed.

"Thattaboy!" said Meg.

Bentley wiped his mouth. "Tastes like chicken."

"Boost me up," said Julie.

"What are you going to do?" said Roman, even as he and Bentley lifted her up to the breach.

"Somehow I need to get Vivian out of my waking mind and back here into Slumberia," said Julie. "But if I do, you guys need to keep her here, so I can take back control of my body and stop my mom from drinking that hot chocolate! You'll probably have to lock her up until the breach heals again."

"Will do," said Roman, just as Julie touched the quivering breach.

It sucked her in like a raw oyster into a greedy mouth.

❩

JULIE WAS standing upright in a gloomy hall of mirrors. *More mirrors!* she thought, for they covered the walls and ceiling, even the floor. They all reflected Julie's image. Most were fun-house mirrors—warped or rippled or elongated—so the surfaces were distorted. Some reflections were silly, where she looked impossibly thin or ridiculously fat. Others were beautiful, where her whole body looked like a kaleidoscope. And a few were downright grotesque, where her face was flattened like a pancake or bulging like a pumpkin.

So this is what my waking mind looks like from the inside, thought Julie. In a way, it made sense. There were times when her mind *felt* like a house of mirrors, with the thoughts bouncing back and forth like little beams of light. And there were times when nothing seemed clear, and everything ended up a little—or a lot!—distorted.

All of a sudden some of the images in the mirrors began to shift and change. *How curious,* thought Julie, since she hadn't moved at all. It was almost as if there were a second Julie along with her in this fun house of mirrors.

Vivian! She was even still wearing the pink bathrobe with the towel around her head!

The black spot—the breach in the wall between Julie's waking and sleeping minds—floated on the surface of a nearby mirror. Julie knew that somehow she had to get Vivian back through it.

"Hello?" Vivian called. "Who's there?"

The images in the mirror moved again. Vivian was coming Julie's way! Julie needed to hide.

Or did she? Julie wondered. Maybe Vivian wouldn't notice her amid the flood of images. Julie stepped back and pressed herself against the surface of one of the mirrors.

She waited, not moving a muscle.

All around her, distorted reflections fluttered and danced.

Then Vivian—the real Vivian!—stepped into view right in front of Julie.

"I *know* you're in here, Julie," said Vivian matter-of-factly. "So come out and show your—"

Julie lunged and pushed Vivian hard—right toward the breach on the surface of the mirror behind her.

"Wha—?" said Vivian.

Vivian slammed back against the black hole, just as Julie had intended.

There was a loud slurping sound as the breach started sucking her inside.

"Ha!" Julie shouted.

But her cry of victory came too soon. At the last second,

Vivian reached out and grabbed Julie by the front of her pajamas. Julie felt herself being pulled into the mirror. She was being sucked back into Slumberia too!

"Nooo!" Julie screamed, but it was too late.

)

JULIE AND Vivian reappeared in the air over the creative juices tank, then fell to the tank and landed with loud clangs.

Julie immediately scrambled upright. "Quickly!" she said to Roman and her friends. "Boost me back up again! And don't let Vivian follow!"

Roman crouched down to lift Julie up.

Meanwhile, Vivian stood more slowly. She calmly straightened her bathrobe and adjusted the towel still wrapped tightly around her head.

"You're too late," she said softly.

Julie shot her a look. "What?"

"She's dead," said Vivian. "Your mother. She was just about to sip the hot chocolate when you pulled me back in here. By now she must be dying on the kitchen floor."

"That's a lie!"

Vivian smiled smugly. "Suit yourself."

"I can still call an ambulance!" said Julie. She let Roman start to boost her up.

"Here we go," he said, grunting.

"Stop!" Vivian said.

Vivian had grabbed Meg by the neck. The glowworm hung limply down from between her fingers like a giant unfilled balloon.

"Stand down," Vivian said. "Let me go back where I was, and I'll let the worm live. Keep going, and she dies."

"Keep going, Julie!" Meg wheezed. "Don't mind—"

Vivian squeezed her throat closed, cutting Meg off in midsentence. The worm's eyes bulged, and her face, already pale, went stark white.

"Wait!" Julie said to Vivian. Julie stepped down from Roman's hands. "Let Meg go, okay?"

Vivian loosened her grip on Meg. "That's *much* better," she said. "Now I'm going back through the hole. And if you ever try to follow me again, I'll make sure your father dies too. I don't really need him anymore anyway."

"But—"

"Just back away from the hole! All of you. I want you all standing on the other side of the tank."

Julie, Roman, Bentley, and the dreamwriter did exactly as Vivian asked.

"Now," Vivian said, "once I'm—"

Suddenly Meg twisted around in Vivian's hands and slapped her in the face with the tail end of her body.

"*Ouch!*" said Vivian. Surprised by the slap, she let the worm drop, and Meg quickly wiggled away.

Vivian stumbled backward—onto the sloped edge of the creative juices tank.

"Oh, that was *not* smart!" she hissed.

"Vivian, be careful!" said Julie. "You're too far out. Here, give me your hand." She took a step forward and reached out to Vivian.

"Oh, please!" said Vivian. "I don't need—"

The towel around her head suddenly unraveled. She started to totter backward. She had lost her balance, so it was too late to grab Julie's hand now. Her eyes bulged. Her arms swung wildly in circles.

Suddenly her face got very calm. "Well, I did always want to do a death scene."

Then she fell straight back off the edge of the tank.

She screamed as she fell.

Down.

Down.

Down.

She hit the concrete below with a sickening thud. Her scream stopped so suddenly it was like it had been cut with an ax.

Julie and her friends slowly crept closer to the edge of the tower, peering down to the ground below.

"Is she . . . ?" Julie asked.

"Not to worry," said the dreamwriter. "Vivian's survived a lot worse than that. You should read some of her early dream-reviews. No, I have a feeling you haven't seen the last of Vivian Clavier."

"Does that mean I'll be coming back to Slumberia someday?" Julie asked.

"Count on it," said the dreamwriter.

"But how do you know? How can you be so sure?"

"Hey, I'm the dreamwriter, remember? I know an obvious sequel when I see it."

"Julie," Roman said. "Your mother. You can still save her."

"You're right!" Julie said. Roman boosted her up to the hole in the air. "Goodbye, Meg!" she said. "I'm so glad you got a chance to travel! And goodbye, Bentley! I'm going to miss your legal advice!" She looked at Roman with tears in her eyes. "And I think I'll miss you most of all!"

"Just go," he said, lifting her up and shoving her roughly into the breach.

14

Dreamgirl

JULIE OPENED her eyes. She was back in the "real" world, but lying on the floor in the middle of the kitchen. Her mother and father looked down at her with concern.

Julie bolted upright. "Don't drink the hot chocolate!"

"What?" her mother said.

"Did you?"

"Julie—"

"Just answer me! Did you drink the hot chocolate yet?"

"No," her mother said. "I was just about to when you fainted."

Julie looked over at the table and saw two mugs of hot chocolate, both full. She sighed in relief. Apparently, when she had pulled Vivian back into Slumberia, there had been no one operating the waking mind, so her body had collapsed.

Julie scrambled up and snatched the mugs of hot chocolate. Then she poured them down the sink.

"What are you *doing*? That's real Swiss chocolate!"

"Mom, you put in too much orange zest. Trust me on this."

"Julie, honey," her father said. "Are you sure you're all right? Your mother said you took a pretty bad spill."

"I'm fine." She faced them. "But Dad, I'm afraid I've got some bad news. I can't do your show."

"*What?*" Her dad looked a little like he was going to faint himself.

"It's the nerves," Julie said. "I just can't handle it. That's why I fainted just now."

"*See?*" Julie's mom said to her dad. "I *told* you she didn't really want to do it! Julie, let me make you some more hot chocolate. Just wait till you taste the fresh mint!"

"Julie," her dad said, his voice catching nervously. "Now, let's not be rash, okay? I don't think I told you that our lead-in has gone syndie, and our ancillary is top four!"

"I'm sorry, Dad, no. And Mom, no thank you on the hot chocolate."

"Apple cider, then!" said her mom. "As you know, I use fourteen different spices in my spiced cider."

"She doesn't want any cider!" her dad snapped. "What she wants is a bigger piece of the back end. That's it, isn't it, honey?"

Julie's father stared eagerly at her. She couldn't get over how familiar this felt, once again being caught between them and being asked to choose sides. Julie wondered what had happened to his promise to try harder to get along. It was as if the whole adventure in Slumberia had never happened.

But then, it *hadn't* happened to her parents. It had happened to her.

"Julie?" her mom said. "What about the cider?"

"Or your own spinoff!" her dad said. "Or you could cut a CD!"

It *had* happened to her. Julie had been to Slumberia and taken on the dream-producer, the Trull, the dream-executives, even Vivian. And she'd beaten them all. As a result, Julie now knew that she wasn't powerless in the face of anything.

"This is between you two," Julie said to her parents. "In the meantime, I'm going to bed."

)

CHRISTMAS LIGHTS *twinkled on a tree surrounded by piles of presents. Carols were playing in the background, and the air smelled of cinnamon and fresh oranges.*

Julie's parents sat together on the couch holding hands.

"Julie?" her mother said. "Would you like some eggnog? The key is fresh-ground nutmeg from a nutmeg grinder."

"Why, thank you," said Julie, taking a glass.

"This is so wonderful," said Julie's dad. "I feel happier than a show-runner with a twenty-six share."

Julie had no idea what her father had just said, but she smiled anyway. "Dad, I couldn't agree more."

The doorbell rang.

Julie stood. "I'll get it! I bet it's my friends."

She went to the front door and opened it.

"Roman!" she said. "And Meg! Bentley! And Lisa! Come in, come in!"

Roman, Bentley, and Julie's best friend Lisa carried gifts wrapped in glittery paper. Meanwhile, Meg held a candy cane in her mouth.

"Mom? Dad?" said Julie, turning to her parents. "Lisa's here with the new friends I was telling you about."

"How lovely!" said Julie's mom, not reacting at all to the fact that a giant glowworm and a talking shark had just entered her living room.

Roman pulled Julie to one side. "I was watching through the mirror," he said. "Things looked pretty rough with your parents back home. You okay?"

Julie beamed. "I'm absolutely terrific." She turned to the others in the front room. "Now, what say we all open our gifts?"

ACKNOWLEDGMENTS

THIS BOOK would not exist without the tireless efforts of four people: my editors, Jonathan Schmidt and Susan Chang; my agent, Jennifer DeChiara; and my partner since 1992, Michael Jensen. If you didn't like it, blame them.

A special thanks to my always willing (and sometimes ruthless) first readers: Laura Williams McCaffrey, Marcy Rodenborn, Melanie Rigney, and Claudia Riiff Finseth.

Dreamquest was written with the assistance of a Grant for the Development of a New Work, given by the Seattle Arts Commission.

DREAMQUEST

TALES OF SLUMBERIA

Brent Hartinger

ABOUT THIS GUIDE

The information, activities, and discussion questions that follow are intended to enhance your reading of *Dreamquest*. Please feel free to adapt these materials to suit your needs and interests.

ABOUT THE AUTHOR

Brent Hartinger was a writer from the start, publishing his own newspaper, the *Weekly Worm,* with friends Tom and Tim, from the third through eighth grades. Determined to make writing his adult career, he lived frugally, taking odd jobs and writing freelance. Over a period of fifteen years, Brent wrote eight novels, twelve plays, fifteen screenplays, and many short stories. His breakthrough came with the 2003 publication of *Geography Club* (HarperCollins) followed by sequels *The Order of the Poison Oak* (2005) and *Split Screen* (2007). Other books include *The Last Chance Texaco* (HarperCollins, 2004) and *Grand & Humble* (HarperCollins, 2006). Frequently named Book Sense Picks, TeenReads.com Best Books, and ALA Quick Picks for Reluctant Readers, Brent's novels have been cited on such award lists as IRA Notables, Lambda Literary

Award Finalist, and Booklist Top Ten First Young Adult Novels. His plays have been produced nationwide, and he has several screenplays optioned and in development, including a film version of *Geography Club*. Brent is a cofacilitator of Oasis, a gay teen support organization; a cofounder of Authors Supporting Intellectual Freedom (AS IF!); and a faculty member of the Vermont College Writing Program. On his Web site, Brent notes that one of the best things about being a writer is "having people say they liked or were somehow touched by your work. It just never gets old." Mr. Hartinger and his partner, novelist Michael Jensen, live near Seattle, Washington.

WRITING AND RESEARCH ACTIVITIES

I. WORDPLAYS AND UPSIDE-DOWN CLICHÉS

A. The author turns the life of the mind into a three-dimensional adventure by transforming such phrases as "creative juices" into a literal sea and embodying such clichés as "lawyers are sharks" in characters such as Bentley, a lawyer who is, literally, a shark. Make a list of other examples of wordplay used in the story.

B. Go to the library or go online to find several definitions for Julie's last name, Fray. Write a short essay explaining how one or more of these definitions makes sense in terms of what is happening to her character.

C. Can you rearrange the letters of "Alucard" (the castle's name) to make another word that describes the count? What words can you form from the letters of "Vivian Clavier" that describe this character? Find a definition for the literary term "anagram," and discuss how anagrams, and other types of wordplay, are used in the novel.

II. DREAMS AND DREAMERS

A. Write a short essay describing a dream or nightmare you have experienced. Include as many details as you can remember. Were there colors, sounds, or textures? Was there a problem you were trying to solve? Were characters from your real life part of your dream? When and where were you sleeping when you had this dream? Did the dream have any relationship to events taking place in your life at the time?

B. Live a dream. With friends or classmates, create a dramatic presentation based on the dream you described in the exercise above. Or bring to life a scene from *Dreamquest*, using live actors, puppets, or computer animation techniques. Present your "living dream" play or movie to an audience if possible.

C. Imagine *Dreamquest* is being made into a movie. Using pencils, pastels, or other art media, draw several costume or set designs for favorite scenes and characters from the novel. Be sure to note the page numbers of the descriptive passages from the text that inspired your drawings.

III. REALITY WRITES (AND BLOGS)

A. Imagine you have found your way in Count Alucard's castle and are looking into the "Mirror of the Minds." How did you get to the castle? What do you see in the mirror? Write a short story describing your experience.

B. In the character of Roman, write a letter or journal entry describing how you feel about your job and/or how meeting Julie has helped you or changed the course of your life in Slumberia.

C. Design an imaginary blog for Bentley, Meg, Constance, Vivian, or another *Dreamquest* character. Include an autobiographical description, list of goals, postings, a list of pictures or Web links you would include, and any other information you imagine this character would include. Make sure to give the blog a fun name.

QUESTIONS FOR DISCUSSION

1. Where does the author place Julie in the very first sentence of the novel? How does this image help readers understand her character? If you had one sentence to place yourself as a character within a dream, what sentence would you write?

2. How does the author use Julie's parents' careers to show the ways in which they battle for her loyalty and affection? How does Julie feel about her parents' jobs? How does Julie's family situation affect the rest of her life?

3. How is waking in Slumberia different from an ordinary dream? What are Julie's first reactions to this new environment? What does she decide to do?

4. List the stops Julie makes on her journey to the offices of the dream executives. Who does she meet along the way? Are these many stops important? Why or why not?

5. Who is Vivian Clavier? What has she done with the Creative Juices? Compare and contrast the characters of Vivian and Julie. Are they exact opposites of each other? Explain.

6. What does Vivian do to Julie's "real life"? How does this add to the seriousness of Julie's situation? Why doesn't Julie simply rush back to the Creative Juices tank instead of continuing her search for the dream executives?

7. Make a list of the inventive creature and place names, such as grognits, Mount Quintessence, and The Neuronal Swamp, used in the novel. How does the author use playful or metaphoric language to add dimension to his story?

8. What are at least two ways to interpret the title of chapter ten, "The Bottom Line"? Why do you think the author titled the final chapter "Dreamgirl"?

9. How does Julie help to change Slumberia? Describe how her actions change the landscape. What happens to the residents of Slumberia?

10. Does Julie complete her quest before moonset? How does she escape from Slumberia? What happens to Vivian? What, if anything, is different now?

11. In chapter one, Julie observes that "Dreams were like parents, where you didn't have any control whatsoever." Do you agree or disagree? At the end of the story, how might Julie feel about this early statement?

12. Has Julie's "dreamquest" been just a dream? Explain your answer.